LEAGUE OF ELDER
STENIBELLE

THE 3RD TURN OF THE SHADOW TECH GODDESS

REN GARCIA

Loconeal Publishing
Amherst, OH

STENIBELLE

This book is a work of fiction. The names, characters, places, and events in this novel are either fictitious or are used fictitiously. Any resemblance to actual events or persons is entirely coincidental.

Loconeal books may be ordered through booksellers or by contacting:
www.loconeal.com
216-772-8380

Loconeal Publishing can bring authors to your live event.
Contact Loconeal Publishing at 216-772-8380.

Published by Loconeal Publishing, LLC
Printed in the United States of America

First Loconeal Publishing edition: July 2015

Visit our website: www.loconeal.com

ISBN 978-1-940466-30-9 (Trade Paperback)

Also by Ren Garcia

The League of Elder Series:
Sygillis of Metatron
The Hazards of the Old Ones

The Temple of the Exploding Head Trilogy:
The Dead Held Hands
The Machine
The Temple of the Exploding Head

The Belmont Saga
Sands of the Solar Empire
Against the Druries

Turns of the Shadow tech Goddess
The Shadow tech Goddess
Stenibelle

For more please visit: www.theleagueofelder.com

LIST OF ILLUSTRATIONS

Stenibelle, Lady of Belmont-South Tyrol *(Eve Ventrue)* Prologue

Hannah-Ben Shurlamp *(Carol Phillips)* 23

The VUNKULA *(Carol Phillips)* 41

Accosted by Hookers on Hoffman Plate *(Fantasio)* 47

Lt. Gwendolyn, Lady of Prentiss *(Eve Ventrue)* 52

A-Ram and Alesta *(Eve Ventrue)* 58

Melazarr of Caroline *(Carol Phillips)* 110

The Battle in the Hold *(Kayla Woodside)* 168

TABLE OF CONTENTS

Prologue   1
1—Release from Hagthorpe   2
2—Hannah-Ben Shurlamp   15
3—Bolabungs and VUNKULAS   32
4—Planet Fall   43
5—A-Ram and Alesta Return   57
6—The Demophalon John   70
7—All Alone   83
8—Crew in Limbo   101
9—Saving the *George Parr*   120
10—The Statue Moved   136
11—Captured   145
12—Ambush   160
13—Remm Deckard   166
14—Prentiss   177
Epilogue   180
Author Information   181

PROLOGUE

B el leaned back against the padded seat of the open-air coach. The great chestnut horse pulled the coach down the lane and its hooves made a steady *clack, clack, clack* on the country pebble stones.

The countryside moving past the coach was rolling and green, marred only by the narrow road and the occasional ruin decorated in fallen, mossy stone. A distance away a broad azure river flowed in its well-travelled banks. The Zenon-lands in the south of Kana was a place far removed from the constant technological movement of the League.

A small package wrapped in metallic gold paper topped with a lacy pink bow sat on the seat next to Bel. Bel had searched all over for the item within the package. It was expensive and difficult to locate, but well worth the effort and the price.

The arrival of this sunny day was worth it for many reasons.

The peaceful, landlocked countryside passing by was so different from Bel's home by the sea in Tyrol, a noisy place pounded by ocean, occasionally angry, waves and frequent overhead League traffic.

Here, other than the hoof falls of the horse and the coy whisper of wind, there was sweet silence.

A great manor draped in greenery appeared far down the lane. Bel's heart fluttered with anticipation. It had taken Bel a long time to get to this place, both physically and spiritually, but, now that the end of the journey was at hand, Bel thrilled with the prospects of what was to come.

Bel picked up the package and held onto it as the carriage entered the manor grounds.

1—Release from Hagthorpe

The door to the cell opened and stale light streamed in.

"Prisoner Belmont, you've got a visitor," the guard said as he unlocked the door and stepped in. He carried a Hertamer heat rifle, but had it hanging in a casual manner at his side. It wasn't even powered on; the weapon did not make its usual tell-tale buzzing sound when activated. The prisoners in this particular ward weren't considered dangerous or an escape risk, and a weapon was, generally-speaking, a formality.

Belmont had been asleep in the small, uncomfortable bed pushed up against the bare naked wall. It was just past six bells, quite an early time of the morning, and there was usually no rising until ten bells when the prisoner was expected to perform duties in the Ward cafeteria.

"Please wake up," the guard said in a kind voice.

The prisoner hadn't been expecting anybody. Belmont's father often visited when his Fleet ship was near. Being an esteemed Fleet captain, he could loudly side-step the usual prison regulations and visit whenever he wished. The rather large throng of Belmont's sisters, too, visited on occasion, though they had to navigate the yards of red-tape and other demands imposed by the prison. A few of Belmont's sisters publicly stated their strong disapproval of this situation and disavowed Belmont all together. Virginia and Lyra, the two closest sisters, remained loyal at least. Belmont's heart would have been broken otherwise. Lyra and Virginia were the most loved of all.

"Who is it? One of my sisters?" the prisoner asked in a dreamy, sleep-filled voice.

"Don't know. Go on, get dressed." The guard patiently waited as Belmont stretched and got out of bed. He turned away for a moment as the prisoner dressed in the modest prison garb of somber white linens.

The cell was dirty white, small, and empty save the small bed, a modest writing table and a chamber pot. The cell lacked a modern commode. A tiny window looked out on the brown courtyard below. The prisoner continued dressing as the guard patiently waited, stepping into baggy articles of clothing and buttoning buttons.

"I'm done," Belmont said. The floor was freezing; there were no shoes allowed the prisoners, an old prison rule that had never been discarded. "May I have a moment to attend to my hair? I've been sleeping and I'm certain it's a sight."

"You look fine," the guard said casting an approving eye. "Come along. Your visitor is waiting."

The guard escorted Belmont out of the prison complex into the yard. The ground was stony and a little jagged. With no shoes the prisoner winced a little with each tentative step.

The guard noticed. "Do you want some slippers, Bel? I think I can manage to get you some?"

"No, no. Thank you. I'm fine." The prisoner was determined to simply ride it out and endure the pain.

Outside, the glossy cyan sky of Brindval glistened in mid-day sheen. There were no walls around the Hagthorpe Prison complex; no moats, no towers, no stockade. The whole brownstone campus was situated in a tumbled fashion atop one of Brindval's famous "Flying Rocks", literally a large mass of stone that floated high above in Brindval's magical sky.

"The rocks float due to a high concentration of brindacite ore, which repels the iron strata of the planet surface below," Belmont had been told once by the guards as if a tourist on holiday seeing the sights and not a prisoner bound there by law.

Hagthorpe Prison was situated square in the center of the Southern Swarm, a massive cluster of floating rocks of varying size that stretched off into the horizon for thousands of miles. Hagthorpe's rock was a little over two miles square and teetered from north to south at a regular basis. It wasn't wise to venture too close to the edge past the flashing warning posts as the feeling of tilt was most pronounced there; a long fall awaited.

Beyond the perimeter, a small but ever-present squadron of Brindval hunter rocks orbited, waiting for any who might actually try and escape via Gift, confederate, or other smuggled technology. They were nothing more than fairly small Flying Rocks fitted out with engines and thrust exhaust so that they could be piloted, turned and raised up a bit.

Belmont was led to a small courtyard. A man in a simple black suit awaited. His drab attire matched the drab surroundings.

He rustled and appeared rather ill as the prisoner and the guard approached. The guard stepped back and turned on his Hertamer. "Prisoner, bow and present yourself."

Belmont squared and bowed as commanded. "Good sir, I am . . ."

The man interrupted. "I know who you are." He cleared his throat and pulled a handkerchief from his coat. He dabbed his sweating forehead. "The motion of this Elder-Down rock is going to be the death of me."

Belmont and the guard glanced at each other in a knowing fashion; only those of the weakest constitutions were made sick by the ever-present wobble of the rock.

"Shall I summon a bit of calming medication for you, good sir?" the guard asked.

The man considered it a moment. "No, no . . ."

The prisoner chimed in. "If you have any menthols on you, sir, smoking them occasionally helps calm the system."

The man nodded and reached into his coat, pulled out a silver case and opened it, revealing a neat line-up of brownish menthols tucked inside. He selected one with slightly shaking fingers, as the rock gave a slight lurch. He dropped his menthol and the case, the contents spilling out and rolling in random directions. He was clearly flummoxed.

"Guard, where is my coach?"

"In a standard parking orbit. Visitor's vehicles are not allowed to remain parked on prison grounds."

"Please, inform my coach to make ready to return for me at once. I shan't be long." He turned a flaccid shade of green and sucked in his breath as the rock shuddered. He tried to compose himself as he turned to the prisoner. "I am Ottoman John, Esquire, here on behalf of my client."

"And who might that be?" the prisoner asked with a bit of dismay. "Am I being paneled again?"

"No, no. My client is, unnamed at this time and . . ."

The rock began its regular tilt to the south and Ottoman John reacted badly. He fell down to all fours and was on the verge of becoming sick from the motion. Belmont and the guard both had their "Hagthorpe Heels" and felt virtually nothing. They shared a quiet laugh at his expense.

His head lolled between his shoulder blades, Ottoman John spoke in a strangled voice into the stony ground. "Guard, please fetch my coach and give me a few minutes with this person!"

"That shall violate prison rules, sir," the guard replied.

"Sir, Prisoner Belmont is an inmate of Ward 4—a low-risk, minimum security wing," Ottoman John croaked. "The prisoner in question has maintained an exemplary record throughout. Additionally, per the *Secure Laws and Procedures of the Exalted Prisitorium of Hagthorpe Bism, 19th edition*, rule 11457, paragraph 2, section 4 states, and I quote: prisoners displaying no marks of unruly and disciplinary behavior and occupying . . . Wards 4 through 8 may be afforded twenty minutes of assured privacy with a duly processed visitor, provided the 'visitor', which, in this case is me, 'understands all procedures and notices of danger.'"

"Yes, thank you," the guard said. "I am aware of the standing prison rules on the matter, however, rule 11457 pertains to *conjugal visits*. Are you here to have a conjugal encounter with Prisoner Belmont? I'll remind you, sir, this prison is not a whore house."

The guard seemed most protective of the prisoner.

"No, most certainly not," Ottoman John objected. "The rule *assumes* a conjugal nature to the visit, however, there is no specific wording requiring it. Now then, I have twenty minutes. Get my damn coach."

The guard bowed and walked away, "I shall bring this up before the next convened Board of Corrections and Notations and the wording of the rule shall be clarified. We shall not have this issue again." The guard continued on, assuming a watchful position at a far wall and sent for the sick man's vehicle as requested.

Ottoman John rose weakly to his knees. Belmont laughed and picked up a few of the man's menthols as they rolled about on the ground. "Here, sir. I'm sorry you lost your menthols," the prisoner said holding them out.

He took a sweaty breath and gently took them. "Thank you. My time is short and this rock is not to my liking, so I shall be direct. You are interred here for no less than ten years by prison counting due to your theft of the Main Fleet Vessel *Seeker* seven months ago. Is that correct?"

"I maintained my innocence."

"Yes or no, please."

"Yes. I was the duly appointed commander of the *Seeker*, and the Admiralty of the Fleet sought to steal my paid monies and pull the command chair out from under me with malice and intent. And, for that, I was paneled, censured, found guilty and sentenced."

Ottoman John appeared unsympathetic. "Such things happen. This is not a world for the timid, is it? The Fleet Admiralty enjoy a bit of theatre now and again, don't they? If you want something, my dear, you must stretch out your hand and take it, no matter what it is." Ottoman John, green, sweating, bleary-eyed looked up at the prisoner. "You are a beaten down person, are you not, Belmont. You . . . you . . ." His voice hitched and he vomited.

Belmont stepped back. Unshod, the prisoner wished to avoid his expanding pool of sick clogged with the unidentifiable remains of his breakfast.

When Ottoman John finished he stood on shaky legs, still holding the menthol sticks in his hand. "Are you overly attached to this place, Prisoner Belmont? Have you a fondness for tilting ground and pointed guns?" He leaned against the wall.

"I don't understand your question."

Ottoman John was near his end. Overhead, the welcome sight of his vehicle soared past and landed in the reception compound several buildings away. The man was jubilant. "At last. Yes or no, my dear—do you want out of this place or not?"

"Yes, of course, though I am fond of my guard."

"And you'd enjoy an opportunity to clear your name?"

"Yes, of course."

He stumbled away. "Guard!" he called, "I am finished with this prisoner!"

The guard quickly came forward and took the prisoner back to the Ward.

∗   ∗   ∗   ∗   ∗

Two weeks later, Prisoner Belmont was ushered from the tiny cell in the middle of the night, allowed to clean up a little, and brought into a briefing area lit up in sterile white lights. There the prisoner was interviewed at length by an assemblage of administrative officials and presented, item, by item, with personal possessions that had been confiscated upon internmen::

A black, Vith-style hat.

A pair of registered LosCapricos weapons known as NTH's

A small box of cinnabar striker plates.

A nickel-plated Grenville 40 pistol (Bullets removed and bagged by prison staff.)

A white silk blouse.

A black pair of Tyrol leggings, size: small.

A pair of Tyrolese boots, also size small.

Ancillary bits of clothing: socks, undergarments, brassiere and a green silk sash.

A moneybag containing twenty-four Belmont sesterces.

A long green coat of Hoban terlamane with HRN riveted on the collar.

The administering officials were confused. Most of this clothing appeared to be men's clothing, albeit of small size. They wanted to know if they had the correct items. The prisoner, dressing, assured them they were.

The prisoner was given a moment to finish, and then was made to sign a host of documents, both holographic and on paper. That done, Belmont's file was stamped "CLOSED". Belmont was ushered out to the main prison skyport. At the end of the softly lit rock path a skycar waited.

"Is this craft my passage?" Belmont asked.

Nobody responded. The Skycar's hatches opened and stood waiting.

Newly freed Citizen Belmont hadn't asked any questions during the whole process, and no one had volunteered anything. Apparently freedom was at hand. Belmont should be elated or relieved at least.

However, Citizen Belmont didn't feel much of anything—things were happening too quickly. Belmont had thousands of questions, yet none came to mind. The guard, he'll be missed. He was a good fellow.

Mind blank, feeling somewhat dizzy, Belmont crunched across the yard in Tyrol boots toward the skycar.

Being free meant having to cope with all the things that had happened.

Removal from chair.

Paneling

Public humiliation and trial.

Censuring by the Sisterhood of Light.

Belmont had hoped those troubling things wouldn't have to be dealt with for some time, perhaps not until the sting of it all was lessened through the years. Not enough time had passed, the wounds were still fresh.

Sitting inside the skycar were a man and a woman. They got out as Belmont approached. The man was tiny with sloped shoulders and bright blonde hair. The woman was also small. She wore linen robes of green and red and had a great, pinned-up mass of black hair. She looked like a Pilgrim of Merian, Belmont was familiar enough with their order, playing in the ruins of their old hermitage on the hill with Lyra and Virginia, laughing and giggling, pretending they could see the Merian's Star.

"You see their Star?" Lyra would ask.

"I do. I see it," though Belmont could not see the Star.

"Are you to transport me home? Back to Kana?" Belmont asked.

"We are," the man responded.

A slouchy civilian man and a Pilgrim of Merian were the pilots? An odd pair. Belmont walked past them, climbed aboard and got comfortable in the back.

"All set back there?" the man asked.

"Yes, thank you."

He and the woman climbed in and the man lifted the skycar into the air and through the swarm of floating rocks to the clear sky of Brindval's lower atmosphere. Belmont watched the prison fall away into the distance and settled back for a long trip into space.

"Where am I going?" Belmont asked in a soft voice. "Home? I'm assuming it's home, yes?"

The sting of the conviction, the humiliation of censure and loss of status hit full once again. The raised eyebrows, the disapproving stares.

I did all of this for you, for our House! What actions did you take? What help did I have?

At least, safe and hidden in prison, Belmont was out of the League's eye and was a dead topic. Now, freed, there will be talk and rumors again that Lyra and Virginia and the other Belmont sisters will have to deal with in full. Belmont didn't want that. They had suffered enough.

Perhaps prison was a better place to be. It was a good safe place to hide.

As they climbed skyward, the woman turned back. She reached out and gently touched Belmont on the knee. "How are you, Bel?" she asked.

Bel?

She used Belmont's old nick-name. Belmont looked up and stared at the woman, trying to place her face. She was undeniably pretty; a porcelain-like face with cherub cheeks, soft blue eyes and a comforting smile. Her robes had a homemade look to them. Belmont recognized the styling.

"Are you a Pilgrim of Merian, ma'am?"

"I am, Bel."

Again, the nick-name.

"And, do I know you?"

The small man flying the ripcar turned back. "You know us both, Bel."

Perplexed, Belmont stared hard at the man. He was mousy and slight wearing a tailored brown Calvert suit. He wore an odd pair of lenses on his face. Whereas the woman with black hair sitting next to him was a complete stranger, the small man looked somewhat familiar.

Wait . . .

Yes, Belmont knew this man.

"It's A-Ram, Bel—your helmsman on the *Seeker,* remember me?"

The *Seeker.*

Belmont cringed a bit at the name and all that came with it.

"Oh! Yes, Yes, I remember! I didn't recognize you without the . ."

"My ugly old glasses? Yes, I got rid of those. These ones are much more stylish, wouldn't you say?"

The woman sitting next to him smiled. She had such a pretty smile. "We realize this must be very strange for you, Bel. It's strange for us as well; this is a bizarre realm to be sure. Just, trust me when I say that there is a place where the three of us are very close friends. You saved my life once."

"Did I?"

"Yes. With those NTH's you carry."

Stenibelle laughed. "Oh, did I clock somebody over the head with them in a bar or something? I've never seen a Pilgrim of Merian in a bar."

"It wasn't in a bar, Bel. Oh, I keep forgetting myself. Introductions are in order. My name is Lady Alesta of Dare, 10th order. I am Lord A-Ram's betrothed, and I am also a Pilgrim of Merian, as you just pointed out. In the realm where we come from you are to stand in a very special place at our wedding."

"And what realm is that?"

"It's hard to explain. Suffice it to say that there are many of you and there are many of us as well. This is one realm out of many. Allow me to ask: you've never worn a mask or courted a woman named Lillian of Gamboa, have you?"

Belmont was puzzled. "A mask?"

"Yes. Where we come from, you once wore a mask."

Belmont sighed. "Odd. And, I'm supposed to believe that? Why would I choose to wear a mask? Was I a criminal there, too? Did I accost travelers on the roadway and steal their wares? And, to answer your question, I've never courted a woman, my tastes are not quite so exotic."

A-Ram turned back from the wheel. "You wore a mask, Bel, because it contained magics that protected your soul from being ripped apart. And, there's one other thing you need to know."

"What?"

"In the place where we come from, you're a man."

Stenibelle, Lady of Belmont-South Tyrol could see her reflection in the Skycar's glass: a pretty Belmont face framed with black Belmont hair. It had been a while since she'd seen her own face as there were no mirrors in Hagthorpe. She needed a bit of a haircut; her black hair had a wild, curled edge to it. She could do with a touch of make-up as well. And there were her men's clothes that she wore in public despite the fact she enjoyed wearing her Belmont gowns when at home.

She was going to be the son her father never had, going farther than even her tomboy sister, Lyra.

Stenibelle reared back and laughed hard, holding her hand to her full bosom. "There are no men in the Belmont-South Tyrol line. I am the thirtieth of thirty Belmont daughters. My mother refused my father a son as he would not quit the Fleet, hence, our line is near an end."

"Where we come from, you were born a man, Bel. Your name there is Stenstrom, after your father, and you are the duly appointed captain of the MFV *Seeker*, privateer-wing."

"Sounds like a nice place," Stenibelle said.

"You're also a lot taller as a man. I figured, even as a lady, you'd be taller." A-Ram appeared to be curious. "Tell me, Bel, your NTH's. Do they work for you here? Ladies can't fire NTH's where we come from."

She pulled an NTH from her sash, pointed it at her head and pulled the trigger with a hollow click. The hammer fell and nothing happened. "They do not. These are treasures of our line, they belonged to my grandfather. I simply carry them because I like to. I'd hoped to give them to my son some day when I have children."

Alesta had a question. "Why didn't you try to break out of Hagthorpe, Bel?"

"How could I? I was interred."

"With your Tyrol sorcery?"

"My what? Sorry?"

"Come on, Bel," A-Ram said. "You can pick pretty much any lock you encounter. You're never disarmed with your MARZABLE daggers and you can fade into the shadows and they'd never see you. Of course we know all about it."

Stenibelle was thunderstruck for a moment. These people appeared to have full knowledge of her deepest and most closely held secrets. "You're aware of these things because you know me, correct? Because we're friends you know these things?"

"That's right, Bel."

She was finally convinced these people weren't mad. "All right, then. Why didn't I attempt to escape? I simply wanted to perform my time, blemish-free, and be done with it. My sister, Virginia, advised that course of action at the beginning. Seemed like good advice. Ten years isn't so long, in the greater scheme of things. So I stayed in my cell and was a good girl. Perhaps ten years out, nobody would remember me. I think that's what I wanted most."

Questions began to sort themselves out in Stenibelle's head. "So, how is it that I am a free woman after less than a year?"

Alesta spoke. She had a pleasing voice, tinged with a Barrow accent. "From what we've been told, you have been freed by a professor from the University of Dee."

"A who? Did you say a professor?"

"Yes. Her name is Grand Dame Hannah-Ben Shurlamp, EVoR" A-Ram said. "The fellow you met the other day, Ottoman John, Esquire, is her associate and leg man. She went back through the specifics of your case, found a few minor improprieties and slights in procedure and quickly built the basis of an argument to call your trial null. The Sisters were agreeable with the course of action, and hence, here is your release. A free man, I mean . . . woman. Sorry. We are taking you to a transport which will ferry you back to Kana at her expense. The Sisters helped us get this opportunity to speak to you."

"So then, I suppose I'll ask: why does a professor from Dee have such an interest in me?"

The skycar broke the clouds and A-Ram leveled out a bit, apparently in no hurry to get to where they were headed.

"Hannah-Ben Shurlamp is a professor well known for her many contributions to the various arts and sciences. She is a grand eminence. She's also a ruthless pursuer of fame, a thief, a murderess and a traitor to the League, some say."

"Quite the resume of infamy," Stenibelle remarked.

"We're being serious, Bel."

"I see. So, my question remains unanswered, what does she want with me?"

"She often employs those whom she believes have some skill and little recourse available to them. She knows of your skill with Tyrol sorcery and she knows of the state of your House's affairs. She intends to use you in her most current ambition. The Sisters advise caution, as they love you."

"Now I know you two are off your rig," Stenibelle said, laughing. "The Sisters despise me, as was made evident during the trial."

"Not true," Alesta said. "The Sisters care deeply for you. They made a public show of their displeasure, as with their censure, however they manipulated the proceedings behind the scenes. They also ensured your internment was as comfortable as possible. The Fleet's man wanted you branded as a dangerous felon and placed in Ward 1 where the worst of the lot go. The Sisters prevented that."

"Very kind of them. And why did they bother?"

"Bel, where we come from, you are the Sister's It Man."

"Pardon?"

"It is a man who has the genetic ability to receive the Sisters' power. The Stenstrom we know is incredibly strong, virtually invulnerable, can perform TK like the Sisters and can dispel Shadow tech."

"Fascinating, however, as you can see, I'm not a man and nor am I an 'It Man'. I am not strong. I am not invulnerable. I can barely last a minute against my sister Lyra in a friendly wrestling match. I never could beat her."

Strong?

Invulnerable?

She remembered getting thrown into the sand by her sister Lyra. Stenibelle, the youngest, the smallest, never able to out-wrestle her sister in the sand.

"Get up, Bel," she recalled her sister saying. *"Get up!"*

"The Sisters said that here, you do have some abilities, mostly regarding an imperviousness to time and time alteration—I don't know what the specific import of that is so don't ask."

Stenibelle had no idea what that meant and was tiring of the company. "Well, jolly for me," she said. She closed her eyes and hoped to retreat inside herself.

Jolly for me . . .

Alesta sounded sad. "There's much at work here, Bel, past the surface of things. We are subject to it, as are you, and the Sisters too. There is a doom that could be coming, and they need your help to circumvent it."

She rolled her eyes and tuned Alesta out. She wanted them to go away. She wanted the peace and forgotten solitude of her cell. She stared out the window. "A lot of nonsense," she mumbled.

"In another place, I told you pretty much the same thing, and there you listened," Alesta said.

Stenibelle had enough and her temper came up. She struggled in her seat, the harness digging into her side and galling her. "In another place, I did this, and in another place I did that! What a load of bollix! Perhaps you should go back to that happy place, wherever it is then and converse with a better version of me, in a place where I am a man; an 'It Man'. I want to do nothing but return to what's left of my holdings and become a recluse spinster, shaking my fist at the injustice of the world from the privacy of my own crumbling parlor."

Alesta was saddened. "Bel, I know you've had a hard time of it, but . . ."

"But what? I have been publicly humiliated, incarcerated . . . censured. My money is all but gone defending myself in the courts and my House is soon to be extinct. I tried to go out and make my mark with the small hope of saving our House, and look what happened. What a sorry bit of tabloid news I was, yes? Perhaps my departed mother was correct— Tyrols needn't involve themselves outside of Tyrol. Nothing good may come of it."

"You're only half Tyrol, the other half is Belmont, bold and adventurous."

"Am I?"

Alesta wanted to say something further, but stayed quiet.

They spent the rest of the trip in silence.

2—Hannah-Ben Shurlamp

Long faces and an awkward silence were the order of the day as the ride into space continued. The skycar ascended into the lower atmosphere and linked up with a slow transport in orbit. There, Stenibelle thankfully took her leave from A-Ram and Lady Alesta. They were both clearly disappointed and at a loss for words as she walked away. She didn't even say goodbye.

What of it? She'd become used to disappointing people, people she loved, friends both old and new. It was a habit she'd gotten into. And, who were these two? They were not her friends. Who were they that she needed their consent and approval?

But, what about A-Ram, the kid from the Admiral's office who followed her into space on the *Seeker?*

"I can fly. Been flying all my life."

He had trusted her. And then: *"They're boarding us, Bel! What do we do?"*

Stenibelle muttered to herself as the ugly memories played themselves out in her head once again. "I don't know. What can we do? I'm sorry I got you into this."

"What do we do?"

She remembered A-Ram sitting there in his Calvert suit as she walked away.

I'm sorry I disappointed you, A-Ram. You deserved better.

Her benefactor's generosity continued, first release from prison, now first-class accommodations. She'd been given a lovely room in the first-class section of the transport. It was nice and self-contained and, most importantly, all expenses paid. That was important as Stenibelle was all but a newly-hatched pauper.

She stayed in her room, not partaking of the general meals and occasional camaraderie of the common area. The one time she did come out to fetch a second helping of desert, a gentleman in a Remnath suit saw her and wished to strike up a conversation. He offered her a cigarette.

"Look at you, Bel, you're so cute. The gentlemen simply adore you," Virginia liked to say. *"You could court any you wished . . ."*

She was in no state to be social. She wanted nothing to do with this man or anybody else. She refused his cigarette.

She sat in her room and watched the stars go by, freed from prison, but still very much a prisoner of her shame.

Her thoughts spun.

Lt. Gwendolyn of Prentiss, the tall Zenon woman from the Fleet who came to take her ship. She bristled at the thought of her.

"Lady Belmont, I hereby relieve you of your chair and remand you immediately into Fleet custody for theft and malfeasance of command. And, on a personal note, you could have at least made this difficult for me."

The transport made its lazy way from Brindval to Kana over the course of two days, Stenibelle's mood matching the pace of the journey. As it settled into a high orbit, there was a knock on her door. She meekly answered. "Yes?" she quietly asked.

Standing at her door was Ottoman John, this time looking much more at ease than he had on Hagthorpe, apparently the stuffy surroundings and manufactured air of the transport was much more to his liking. "Lady Belmont, it is good to see you again. I have summoned a footman to attend to your things. If you would, may I entreat you to follow me?"

"Sir Ottoman, not quite so green this time out. Pity—I thought the shade suited you."

Had Stenibelle said that or just thought it? She wasn't sure. Ottoman John didn't react one way or another, so she must not have said anything.

"Come this way, please." Stenibelle was used to the regimented life in prison, and Ottoman's request had the sound of an order. She came out of her room, popped on her hat and followed Ottoman John without a word or thought of protest.

As she followed him through the ship, her previous conversation with Lady Alesta and A-Ram flashed through her mind. "Where are we going?" she asked.

"To see your benefactor."

"And, who is that?" If A-Ram and Alesta were not utterly mad and had told her the truth, then she already knew the answer: a strange professor from Calvert awaited her at the end of this journey.

"Please, we've a schedule to maintain. All shall be made plain in short order."

"Fine, no vomiting." Once again, she thought witty things but didn't bother to say them.

They stepped into a waiting ripcar and quickly were out the transport and on their way down to Kana below. Stenibelle sat in her seat quietly, still hearing the raised voices of her detractors that had assailed her during the trial.

"A disgrace and a traitor . . ."

"The worst and most ill-thought out appointee in recent memory. We shall re-write the book based on this disaster."

"If you weren't a lady, I'd call for your head!"

She, sitting there on the stand, listening to the searing words, seeing her father sitting in the gallery, the memory of it all pained her as if it had just happened.

"I'm sorry, father. I did my best."

As the ripcar dropped into the atmosphere, Stenibelle could see the long golden line of the eastern coast tracking from south to north. About midway up was the spur of land jutting into the water where Tyrol was located.

Tyrol, Belmont Manor, her home. She wanted to go home, to bask in it and be soothed by all the things she loved, but the ripcar veered south, to the briny spit of land east of the Great Armenelos forest. It was a curved bit of ochre.

Calvert. The ripcar veered to the west and soon was skimming the treetops of the forest; dark green and primordial, bursting with life. A craggy graystone manor, plunked somewhere in the tangled growth jutting above the trees, appeared at a rapid pace. The Ripcar settled into a tenuous clearing landscaped and studded with fountains and pathways. Containment came down and Stenibelle got out. Several servants ushered her onto a central path, passing not one but two string quartets, wigged, hosed, and dressed for success; spilling sweet, cultured music into the afternoon air amid the cawing and flapping commotion of the forest perimeter beyond. Gardeners hauled wheelbarrows full of shorn vegetation away. Keeping the massive forest at bay was clearly a daily chore. Winged, reptilian beasts lurked at the fringes of the compound, occasionally shaking the branches.

Stenibelle, despite the sweet music and manicured lawns, thought she could hear the wild forest stretching and growing around her.

Wigged footmen in frills, buckle shoes and pastel coats came forward to receive her. She was whisked down a footpath to the cool, temperature-controlled interior of the manor. Clattering on marble and polished stone, she was led through enameled corridors under paneled ceilings and painted hangings.

Somewhere down a quiet wing, a heavy door opened for her. A spacious chamber, ornate and splendid, waited within. "If you will, my lady, fine garments have been laid out for you," the footman said. "Please, we entreat you to put them on. Do you require assistance?"

Stenibelle could see a lovely gown draped over a mannequin waiting within, accompanied by flanking mannequins holding trays bearing fine linens and knickers and a pair of jeweled shoes. "Of course I don't need any assistance."

"Excellent, women of Tyrol are so independent, so I've been told. If you would then?" The footman motioned for her to enter.

She stepped inside and the heavy door shut behind her. Standing in the baroque room livid with finery she heard the mags slide and engage. Locked in. She'd come all this way just to be imprisoned again. She could pick the lock and be out, if she wanted. She could fade into the shadows and not be seen as her Mother had taught her. Before the trial, she would have done those things. She would not have stood there in a strange manor locked in an unfamiliar room, fabulous, certainly, but no less a prison than her bare cell in Hagthorpe. Before the *Seeker*, Lady Stenibelle would not be bound.

Instead, she was now the post-*Seeker*, post-trial Stenibelle. The beaten one. The disgraced, incompetent one her Mother, thankfully, hadn't lived to see.

"I hereby order you to come about, stand clear and await my boarding . . ."
The one who did as she was told.

Obediently she took her HRN and boots off, carefully laying them out on table where automated mannequins came and spirited them away, brushing the material as they went. The mannequins were geared and tautly cabled, some being full human automatons clicking with precision movement and preprogrammed grace, others were wheeled and only partially human-like and others were just delicate appendages running on mounted rails. Off came her man's pants and her frilly white blouse— more mannequins took those. She let her Vith triangle hat fall to the floor; it didn't remain there long. Another mannequin bore it away.

There she was standing there in the guilded mirror; nude. A smallish, black-haired woman, pretty, with an inviting smile, though she wasn't smiling at the moment. Blue eyes like ice—now those were rather striking. The gentlemen calling on her through the years always remarked on her eyes. Good hips, Tyrol hips like her mother had, built for punching out twenty or thirty children. There were the two dotted moons of her breasts and the waiting pearl of her vagina. She was in need of personal grooming to keep things properly in check.

She tried to imagine herself as a man and failed: taller, with muscles, no hips and a cod piece. Couldn't see it. Wasn't possible.

She mused: *If I had a little something dangling there I wouldn't be in this mess, would I? I could have married some tea-drinker. I could have bedded and given her a good pounding every evening and punched-out Belmont heirs left and right. What currency a little hog-leg can offer.*

Water came on in the bath chamber beyond and the mannequins gestured for her to enter and wash. She felt the steam and the heat of the hissing water and smelt the fine oils and expensive soaps awaiting her. Her showers at Hagthorpe had all been cold and sterile.

She saw something lying on the dense carpeting of the floor. It was a small photo, possibly it had fallen out of the pocket of her HRN as the mannequin had carried it away. Where had it come from? She hadn't seen it before. Perhaps those two crazy-people A-Ram and Alesta had put it there trying to stir some sort of nostalgia within her. That must be the case. She picked it up and looked at it.

There, in the photo was a group of people standing together, smiling. She recognized Lady Alesta and A-Ram—they looked to be a very happy and well-suited couple. She envied them a little bit as she gazed at the photo, they had each other and that was all that seemed to matter. Next to them was a tall, handsome man, and near him was a pretty but somewhat proper-looking woman wearing a Fleet uniform with long brown hair. She stood with perfect posture and regal bearing.

That tall man—he was wearing an HRN coat, just like hers, only bigger and longer. It was unmistakable.

He had a Belmont face, like her father and black Belmont hair.

NTH's jutted from his sash.

Eyes blue like ice.

Wait! She sucked in her breath. Was that *her?*

Alesta and A-Ram had said she was a man in another reality. A bunch of balderdash, who wouldn't think so; however, the whole concept of alternate realities wasn't totally new or alien to her. Her Mother, during her years of secret training in Tyrol sorcery in the abandoned culvert under the city, had speculated on the existence of such a thing. And, come to think of it, she'd had occasional distant dreams of being a man, of fighting like a man and firing the NTH's. Of loving women . . .

So, no, being a man in an alternate reality didn't, after some reflection, surprise her much at all. She stood there holding a photo that belonged in another universe, was taken in another universe, depicting people from another universe. Everything seemed pretty normal and familiar, except for him/her. It figured that he/she would be the odd man/woman out.

Perhaps the photo was a fake, and A-Ram and Alesta were out to con her. Con her out of what? Money??

The man in the picture wore a triangle Vith hat like she did, Tyrol boots of leather and silver and wore a green sash with the wooden handles of two pistols that resembled NTHs jutting out. She recognized the detailing on the grips. Those were her grandfather's NTHs, the ones she herself carried though they wouldn't function for her because she was a woman. If A-Ram and Alesta were con artists, then they were master forgers.

Stenstrom the Younger, Lord of Belmont-South Tyrol.

If this photo was to be believed, then in another place, she was a man and therefore her House wasn't doomed. In another place, she hadn't lost her chair and been sent to prison. A-Ram and Lady Alesta hadn't mentioned that; on the contrary, they seemed surprised and put off by her dour attitude and her situation.

They said he was the bonded captain of the *Seeker.*

He had succeeded. That was reason for a bit of hope.

In another universe, perhaps she wasn't an utter, defeated failure. She had a bit of longing for a moment as the water from the shower hissed. Some of her old spirit began to stir. Just like when she was a girl, fruitlessly wrestling with her sister Lyra—always the smaller and the weaker, but not lacking in spirit and determination.

"Get up!" Lyra would say as Stenibelle lay in the sandpit. And, without fail, she always got up to come to grips with her and to try again.

Her eyes fell across the picture to the woman standing next to him—*her*. Who was she? Long brown hair, wearing a female-issue Fleet uniform; a lieutenant. She had rather stern expression for a lady. A rapier dangled from her hip. She'd seen that face before. Where?

Wait! It's her—Lt. Gwendolyn of the *Demophalon John* who boarded her powerless ship and started the chain of events that led to her being unseated, paneled, tried, disgraced and imprisoned.

"Demophalon John coming in to dock. What do we do? Bel, what are we going to do?"

Lt. Gwendolyn, Lady of Prentiss. A woman she hated, truth be told. Look at them standing there; prim and proper, yet there was a familiar closeness to them, as with A-Ram and Alesta. What were they, courting? Romancing?

With her??

Perhaps her alternate male counterpart had little proper taste in women. Hated memories barged into her head.

Hated voices.

"Lady Belmont's ignorance in space-faring was matched only by her souless, uninspirational incompetence as a commander," was Gwendolyn's rather terse testimony on the stand.

She angrily put the photo down and walked into the bathroom. She stepped into the shower and washed, talking to herself as she did so.

"Incompetence? I had a half-scuttled ship and a crew of two. What was I to do?"

Memories intermixed with the rising steam of the water.

"Can we run? Can we fight?"

"We got nothing, Bel!"

She pleaded to no one: "What could I have done?"

"Lady Belmont. I am here to remove you from command and take you into custody."

"Don't let her get away with that, Bel! Knock her out! Knock her teeth out!"

She finished her wash, dried and began the long process of dressing. She stepped into her knickers and linens, pulled on her hose and laced up the corset. She took the gown off the mannequin and laboriously donned it, taking the better part of an hour to get it properly situated around her small body. She then made her face up and put on the heeled shoes. Despite the drudgery, she liked "putting her uniform" on, it brought back happy memories of home when she and her army of sisters got ready for dinner in the vast manor changing room, all of them stepping into garments, pulling corsets tight, pinning their hair up and applying make-up. Many of her sisters were old enough to be her mother and she saw little of them, except in the changing room where all of them together labored to get ready for dinner.

Those same sisters who disavowed her even as she fought to protect their Household and heritage.

Stenibelle was impressed as she brushed on her face. Everything was correct and of the finest quality. The linens, corset and gown were all the proper size. The face paints were all of a shade she favored. The creams enhanced her skin tone. She liked the perfume, and even the shoes fit perfectly. Whoever this Hannah-Ben Shurlamp was, she was meticulous in her details.

Her hair was wild and uncontrollable at the moment, a black, curly mass on her head needing a barber's attention. She tamed it as best she could.

"Look at your hair, Bel," Virginia used to say. *"You resemble a Monama with all that hair. Let me do something with this."* She smiled. Virginia always could make her laugh.

There came a knock a her door.

"You may enter," she said, holding her brush.

The door to the chamber opened as she sat at the boudoir. It was a footman wearing teal and lace. "Good Lady, you are expected at audience," he said. "If you would please . . ."

Stenibelle put down her brush, glided out of the room and followed the footman deep into the interior of the manor. Up a vast staircase, she was led into a colossal study which was baroque enough to have come straight from a dream; colonnades rising up, domes hammered in black and gold, inner terraces and stone walls carved in bold relief.

Sitting behind a gilded hardwood Hoban desk in the center of the room was a woman dressed in a snowy gown of white, gently typing away at a keyboard with one hand and manipulating a large glyph with the other as a tumbling gallery of holographic Icons floated about her head. The glyph looked like a jeweled magic wand and with a flick of it she controlled vast amounts of data. She seemed to be working on at least ten different things at once, each with equal vigor and aplomb. A holo-photo of a portly wigged man floated in a prominent place among the other holos.

She snickered to herself. "Tell your father to watch the bon-bons," she thought. Stenibelle always had a moderately ribald wit, and occasionally embarrassed Lyra and Virginia with off-handed and ill-timed quips when they went to town.

A pink padded chair with dragon-ball feet sat in front of the desk. Stenibelle went toward it and awaited an invitation to sit.

The woman at the desk continued typing and glyphing, sitting quite still and erect save for her fingers which moved in a flurry. She spoke into several cones, her voice muffled. After several minutes she, without looking up, said: "Be seated. I'll be with you in a moment."

Stenibelle sat and gazed at the woman. Though seated, she was clearly tall and fairly buxom. Her skin was powdered to a pearly white and she wore a towering wig of curled locks that looked like a carefully swirled mound of white frosting—almost good enough to eat. A few tendrils of raven-black hair fell out of the seams of the wig and her eyebrows beneath the powder were clearly black. Her eyes, like two brown buttons on a snowy landscape, stood out sharply.

As she waited, Stenibelle felt her humor come up. She decided to speak and break the ice. "Your father is a handsome man," she said, noting the holo-picture of the wigged man floating over her desk. She thought to be bold and ironic, as the man certainly wasn't handsome.

The woman stopped what she was doing. "That, dear lady, is my beloved husband," she said in a regal contralto voice. She began typing again.

"Oh, your pardon." Inside, Stenibelle was roiling in laughter. *What, were they having a sale at the leper farm when you happened by?* She wanted to say it. She wanted to show this woman she was still a confident and bold person.

Without ceasing the pace of her typing or bothering to look in Stenibelle's direction, she spoke. "Doubtless you are aware who I am, and clearly I know who you are, therefore the standard opening pleasantries are irrelevant. Now then . . ."

Stenibelle jumped in, for she felt she'd have little opportunity to speak going forward. "Your pardon, Great Lady. I am not in the habit of speaking to a stranger without proper introductions. I am Lady Stenibelle, 30th daughter, House of Belmont-South Tyrol. And you are?"

The woman stopped what she was doing and appeared rather perturbed. She rolled her glyph over her knuckles and tapped the smooth desktop with her fingernails, making a musical *clack, clack, clack* . . . . Stenibelle felt herself barbequing in the woman's gaze.

"I am Grand Dame Hannah-Ben Shurlamp, Professor Emeritus, University of Dee. EVoR, QrduP. NvPhD. Gran-Sequitor *Hobanis-Realis* and Knight of Bazz. Is that sufficient?"

Stenibelle was certainly impressed. This woman appeared to hold just about every possible merit, title and tenure available to a scholar. Her sister Lyra was currently working on earning her "E" degree from the University of Arden, which had taken her six years of total commitment and still had two or three to go. To become an EVoR would take, at minimum, another hundred and fifty.

"You must be really old then," she wanted to say.

Hannah-Ben Shurlamp resumed her work and spoke. "To answer your first question, which is, no doubt pending, I spent the time and effort to free you from prison because I wish to employ you. I pay quite well, and I am aware your familial monies aren't what they once were. Your House is marking time, isn't it? Which will come first, I wonder, extinction or bankruptcy?"

"Now wait a moment, at least I'm not the one married to a fat guy wearing rouge," rolled through her head. Before Stenibelle could open her mouth and rebut, Hannah-Ben Shurlamp continued. "I wish you to perform a simple infiltration and information gathering session aboard a Fleet vessel. Your skills as a Tyrolese sorceress shall come quite in handy for this particular assignment, and, should those fail, your toothsome pulchritude shall fill in the gaps nicely. Do you understand? The vessel you shall be infiltrating is this one here . . ."

She moved her glyph and the holographic image of a Sprint-class Fleet vessel appeared, slightly spinning; long, pencil-like with a small set of shoulder-mounted wings placed well aft. "The *George Parr*, Sprint-class vessel, *Miranda* variant, captained by Lord Duval of Wilshire in his sixth seating. Captain Duval is a veteran of many campaigns and battles, he is a family man, a sexton at his local church, and he is also a member of the Nillists of Punt."

Stenibelle was about to ask who the Nillists of Punt were when Hannah-Ben Shurlamp cut her off. "The Nillists of Punt are, on the surface, a casual social club, like any one might find and care to participate in around the League, however, a simple query into their club yields a strikingly different picture. They are not of League origins, appear to be quite ancient, and boast members in the League, the Xaphans, Ming Moorland and possibly the odd planet code-named 'Mare' by the Xaphans. Their motto is: *'Se nade mote Crumdie'* which is Old Vith for 'We shall bring about the end of the Universe'."

"They are attempting to bring about the end of the Universe?"

"That is their motto, yes. They believe in a being often called in the usual vernacular the 'Shadow tech Goddess', a fanciful creature powerful enough to destroy everything around her until she is all that is left."

She moved her glyph and an odd carved image appeared in the one of the floating holos. It was a carving of some sort of robed person, probably female, wearing a bullet-shaped, featureless helmet. From the sides of the helmet grew a host of twisting tubes and tentacles. "This is a representation of the Shadow tech Goddess that the Nillists often carry with them. Their goal is to perform certain rites that shall allow for the introduction of the Shadow tech Goddess into this and other realms of being, thereby destroying them."

"For Creation's sake, why?" Stenibelle asked.

"Unknown, and immaterial, as they do not seem to be able to accomplish their goal. There are many destroyers, beings of immense power who are tasked with cleansing certain areas of the universe from time to time, and the Shadow tech Goddess is just one of them." She moved her glyph and the image of the Shadow tech Goddess vanished, replaced by what looked like the raging shaft of a tornado, undulating and terrible. "This is another destroyer, one that I've seen with my own eyes. A cleanser of whole worlds."

She set the glyph down and the image vanished. "But, enough about this. The Shadow tech Goddess and her quaint lore does not interest me in the least. What *does* interest me are certain bits of information the Nillists are gathering in their attempts to summon their deity. That is why you are here."

Professor Shurlamp paused, apparently expecting Stenibelle to interject with a question. She asked none and the professor went on.

"I have it on good authority that the Nillists have stumbled upon the stellar location of long lost Cammara."

Cammara? Stenibelle knew the name. A place of lore, a long forgotten home-world. A place of magic and forgotten dreams. It was . . .

"Yes," the professor said, studying Stenibelle's face. "You know the name and the prospect interests you. Irresistible, isn't it—Cammara. A place of wonder and riches that our ancestors abandoned with the Elders 200,000 years ago during the eponymous CX time epoch. Cammara, like our other former home worlds: Earth, Lemmuria, Emmira, and Eng, is lost to the ages. We followed the Elders, and as they moved on, we moved on too, and Cammara was forgotten. Too much time has passed and its stellar positioning is long since lost. Its light in the sky is unknown. That is an unforgivable offense, to forget knowledge that was once plain simply due to the passage of time. Of course time is the great oblivion, as the Sisters say. All shall be forgotten in time."

"Why not ask your husband, he was probably there," she mused, proud of her unspoken wit. This professor couldn't possibly be serious. "There have been many scholarly efforts to rediscover Cammara, and Eng and the rest. My peer, Professor Merlaman of Shirster, recently gave a symposium regarding his beliefs as to the location of Cammara, and, unfortunately, I had to discredit his claims and humiliate him publically. Even that idiot Professor Compressor from Arden has chimed in on the subject."

Stenibelle stirred. "What does the location of Cammara have to do with the Shadow tech Goddess?" More wry wit bubbled up. *"Shall I take both she and your husband out for a walk?"*

"Apparently, the Nillists believe that certain arcane objects reside on Cammara that shall assist them in summoning the Shadow tech Goddess. My sources tell me that there is a great deal of credibility regarding their research."

"And so, what do you want with me?"

Hannah-Ben Shurlamp momentarily lost her cool, white-powdered demeanor. Her large brown eyes grew wide and she coiled and twisted behind her desk like a great black snake covered in flour. "You," she hissed with intensity, "are going to board the Fleet ship. You are going to observe, ingratiate yourself and listen. That done, you are going to get me the information I seek. You are going get me the stellar positioning of Cammara."

"But . . . I . . ."

"Such knowledge shall set the League on its collective ear. Whomever rediscovers Cammara shall be celebrated forever more as a pioneer and a visionary. Make no mistake, it shall be the name of Hannah-Ben Shurlamp, Professor Emeritus, University of Dee alone, whose name is remembered as the rediscoverer of Cammara. It shall be me who gives the lectures. It shall be me who breaks the bottle on the newly christened Fleet ship dispatched to quest to Cammara for the first time in 200,000 years, and you, Lady Stenibelle, the worthless thirtieth daughter of a dying, impoverished, disgraced Household, are going to fetch me this information. I do not care what needs done. I don't care what beds you have to sleep in, what earlobes you have to bite, what poisons you have to administer, what murders you have to perform, what backs must be stabbed or what graves you must lie in. I shall have this knowledge and you are going to get it for me." She placed her long, somewhat boney fingers on her desktop and moved her nails along the surface. "Am I clear?"

It was like an icy wave had launched itself from across the room and hit Stenibelle full in the face. All her wit and puns regarding the professor's husband dried up and wilted, replaced with shock and a touch of fear. It was like being stuck in a room with her old school master whom she was terrified of. "And, and if I . . ."

"Refuse?" the professor said. "I wouldn't if I were you. Please consider that I have extensive information on not only you, but all of your twenty-nine sisters, and your father and your dead mother too. You must acknowledge by now that I am rather meticulous in my methods. I'll have your sisters defrocked from whatever social circles they inhabit, I'll have your father off his Fleet chair and inhabiting a prison cell at Hagthorpe as you did, and I'll have your mother dug up and set into the stocks in Tyrol where ruffians may throw rotting fruits at her equally rotting skeleton. And, by the by, if it's any interest to you, I could have you right back in Hagthorpe prison alongside your father should I choose to do so, but I think you would rather like that, wouldn't you? Yes, to sit unobserved in a comfortable if Spartan cell where your disgrace can be hidden and forgotten right along with your tiny little carcass. Instead, I think I would go after what's left of your House. I'd call in markers and demand margin calls. I'd bankrupt you and allow your creditors to dissect the worthless remains of your holdings while you watch the entire ordeal from a cricket shack or whatever seedy lodgings you can manage to afford. So, with that in mind, if you wish to be the stake that is hammered into your House's tortured heart at last, then, by all means. . . refuse."

The Professor held Stenibelle locked in a brown-eyed stare for a few moments, then released her and began calmly typing again, her wave of fury passed. "Of course, you also may accept, and be the veritable dove that swoops in and saves your House instead. From convicted felon and public outcast to the grand matriarch of a new House of Belmont-South Tyrol given a fresh lease and awash with new cash. That has a lovely ring, doesn't it?"

Stenibelle struggled to recover, to say something bold and courageous. Could it be true? She had no doubt this woman could do exactly what she said, to save her House and refresh its depleted coffers. She sat up and cleared her throat. Her heart beat with fearful expectation, perhaps getting thrown into prison might be worth it if the end result was the preservation of her House. She tried to offer a word in response, something grand and commanding, something masking her interest and excitement and conveying the illusion of indifference and skepticism as a good business person should, not tipping her hand too soon. All she could manage was: "How?"

"I have information of a previously unknown cousin of your House, and of your mother's House of Tyrol. He is closely related enough, that, should you or any of your sisters be wed to him, then all League rules of heraldry shall be satisfied and your House shall have its male heir at last. Your House and all its holdings shall remain whole and survive this generation and many more to come."

Stenibelle sat there and contemplated it. A male heir at last? The House of Belmont-South Tyrol not lost, but forged anew, and it was the disgraced, youngest daughter Stenibelle who brought its salvation to pass.

Could it be true?

The Professor seemingly read her thoughts and knew the matter was settled. "Yes, you shan't be disappointed. Now, let's to the matter at hand, shall we? I feel, in reviewing your actions during the loss of your chair aboard the *Seeker*, you demonstrated poor leadership skills, appalling seamanship, lack of initiative and a decided lack of imagination. You allowed the Fleet's woman to up and board you without so much as a by-your-leave."

"What was I to do? I had no power, no oxygen and an untrained crew."

"There were a number of things you could have done, you simply didn't do them. And then that Fleet woman from Zenon had you crawling upon the ground."

Stenibelle fought to offer an excuse. "I was under orders." And, she also offered: "She was bigger than me."

"Had she stood between me and something I wanted, she would not be breathing right now I assure you. You lack ferocity, tenacity and ingenuity and you failed to do what needed done. Accordingly, to address these shortcomings, I have left you some necessary tools in your room. I advise you use them. Now, I am going to bathe you in a Ceril-Cone and you shall not forget what is told here."

Stenibelle had many questions. *What is a Ceril-Cone? Is it going to hurt? Should I prepare myself? Wait a moment . . .*

The Professor pressed a button and Stenibelle was washed in a potent pinkish light that came down from above. The light from the Ceril-Cone penetrated deep into her brain, opening it up and holding her in rapt attention. If felt like the top of her head had been lopped off and her brains scooped out, leaving a stringy dry socket.

The Professor spoke in her slow, deliberate manner. "Your instructions are as follows: you are to board the Fleet Sprint ship *George Parr* by whatever means required and apply any necessary pressure to Captain Duval for him to divulge you the location of Cammara. You have four days to prepare, as he shall be set to dock at Hoffman Plate, berthing 77, Planet Fall by week's end. Additional persons of interest to be aware of:

"Lt. Remm Deckard, officially of Carina but secretly from Moedron:

she is captain Duval's first officer, a woman of Famora and occasional lover.

"Rodrigo of Burgon: a Xaphan Warlord and Nillist of Punt heading up the most recent effort to summon the Shadow tech Goddess.

"Melazarr of Caroline 25th daughter of the Xaphan House of Caroline, a Xaphan Tropist and constant companion of Rodrigo of Burgon."

Shurlamp turned the Ceril-Cone down and Stenibelle was free. The information just given to her sorted itself out deep in her thoughts and rooted itself. Lights danced in front of her eyes.

Professor Shurlamp returned to her work, the carnival of holos floating about her head. The door to the room opened and the footman came and escorted Stenibelle away.

"Lady Stenibelle, one more thing," Professor Shurlamp said. "If you don't come up with the information I seek, then don't come up at all."

3—Bolabungs and Vunkulas

She made the long escorted walk back to her room, where, once again, she was locked inside.

Lunch was waiting for her on a sitting table: Steaming hot soup of chicken, rayard meat (a Tyrol delicacy) and rich Tyrol broth, a hot roll made of chewy bead and a light salad. A coffee service with various sugars and creams sat to the side. Again, it was a lunch that was familiar to her; something she might easily have ordered from a cafe for herself.

Once again, Hannah-Ben Shurlamp was on her game, knowing her subject well.

Stenibelle sat alone and ate. It was delicious.

After lunch, she decided to explore her "room" a bit more. She went to the door and tried the latch.

Locked.

She examined it. Though the door appeared to be old and time-worn, its lock was expensive and sophisticated; a mag type, encoded and monitored, and surely would thwart most anybody attempting to crack it.

She waved her hands and produced a small kit of various picks and other tools from thin air. More Tyrol sorcery Professor Shurlamp had touched upon. She guessed she could have this lock picked in under a minute, and in a manner that would thwart the remote monitoring. She'd always been good with her hands, even better at picking locks and moving in the shadows than Lyra and way better than the thick-fingered Virginia.

She waved her hands again and vanished the picks. She didn't bother to try it.

Moving deeper into the room she found a padded alcove sporting a massive canopy bed draped with the finest of fabrics.

Past the alcove was the large bathroom complete with full bath and shower, enclosed commode and sauna. At the end of the room was a small terrace. Her room was situated somewhere in the craggy center of the manor. Battlements and crossing wings rose up all around past the terrace, creating a canyon of brick and ornamented mortar framed in both darkened and lit up glass. She saw the manicured grounds, the elegant walkways and the line of dense growth of the forest beyond, teeming with life struggling and fighting, just waiting to retake these grounds and overgrow it. There were any number of sensing and monitoring devices trained down on her terrace, hidden in all the finery but not escaping her eye. Any attempt to escape would immediately trigger an alarm. She wondered how a fade into the shadows would fare against all of Hannah-Ben Shurlamp's pretty technology. Certainly, the professor knew she could do such a thing, certainly she was prepared for it to some extent.

She wondered, but wasn't interested enough to put it to the test. The professor had her interest peaked and loyalty bought.

To save her House and restore their wealth.

To be, at least in the professor's calculating eyes, vindicated.

Even if her door had been unlocked and her terrace unwatched, she wouldn't have left. She was now, for good or ill, Hannah-Ben Shurlamp's "employee" complete with a Ceril-Coned set of instructions waiting to come bursting out.

She stood out on the terrace a bit longer, watching the evening fade in on the manor and forest beyond. She then returned to the interior of her room and began undressing for bed. As usual, getting the gown off by herself was rough sledding, it being slightly less awkward and confining than a straight jacket.

"Hold still, will you, squirmy?" Virginia used to say.

Eventually, she was down to her linens and knickers. She removed her shoes and set them aside where dutiful mannequins came and took them away, brushing them off and sprinkling scented powder within. She mused what her "male counterparts" would do if they had to spend so long getting ready for each day and then breaking down again at the end of it. Probably wouldn't handle it well. She often favored her HRN and men's clothing; those she could be in and out of in ten minutes.

She seated herself at the vanity and removed her face, yet another time-absorbing labor. She dabbed on salves and liniments, cleansing her

skin and discarding used pads and cotton tissues. Such labor. She thought
of that crazy woman, Lady Alesta, a Pilgrim of Merian who probably
didn't spend ten minutes a day grooming herself, though she recalled her
being very pretty naturally.

Sitting atop the vanity was a wooden chest that hadn't been there
before and a small leather case. She set her cloth aside and opened the
leather case.

Inside was a small but intricate device. Her brains turned to cotton;
Ceril-Cone implanted information came up.

It was a Uni-Mind, an amazing Elder device able to interface and
extract information from any computerized source. There was nothing
to it—simply place the Uni-Mind near the external source and it would
do the rest. With it she could send and receive information, store
information from a variety of sources, and, in some cases, take over less
protected systems. Very handy. She slid it back into the case.

She turned to the chest. Inside, sitting on a black velvet cushion were
five bolabungs of the highest quality. Stenibelle had seen many bolabungs
in her day, had created many herself, but they were always crude,
somewhat smelly contrivances.

These here were ornately carved of ivory, inlaid with micro-fine opals
and lined with hammered gold. She even thought she could see tiny
indications of circuitry built into the ivory and gold with amazing
workmanship. They were shaped into diamonds, stars, ovals and other
arcane shapes.

Stenibelle was impressed.

Bolabungs were, in most cases, haphazard devices made of
wormwood or other sympathetic materials, such as gold, ivory, menthic
or amber and were worn around the neck with a cord, usually of salt-
rubbed leather. In their most basic form, they were intended to shield
one's mind from telepathy and other sorts of unwanted mental
intrusions. Most people carried at least one to provide them with a bit of
privacy in the otherwise mentally verbose League, however, bolabungs
didn't stop there. They could do all sorts of things, depending on their
make and workmanship. They could shield one from arcane eyes, ward
off the effects of menthols and spirits, deaden pain, slow terminal
bleeding and even prevent one from becoming pregnant (making those

sorts of bolabungs "must haves" for courtesans and other pliers of the trades of the night).

And, there was a final thing bolabungs could do. The fabulously expensive ones created by Bolabards of the highest skill, could alter one's basic nature as desired. They could make a stupid man smart or a cowardly man brave. They could coax witty words out of a dull man's mouth and transform a talentless wretch into an artist. Of course, such wonders were not cheap by any means and they were not welcome either; those "Bunged Up" souls once discovered, were disgraced in infamy forever as cheap frauds.

And these five sitting on the black velvet looked to be just that: bolabungs that could transform her into something she was not, a safeguard courtesy her new benefactor and employer, Hannah-Ben Shurlamp.

She got them out of the case and lined them up on the vanity.

There was a mostly sapphire one inscribed with the Vith word: *abnojax*

There was a lovely ochre one inscribed with: *crixamp*

There was a serpentine one of coiled beauty with: *ventross*

There was a garnet wonder inscribed with: *verapones*

And an imposing obsidian masterpiece with: *fenve*

Stenibelle didn't know Vith; an odd language from the north of Vithland. She turned on a nearby holo-terminal and waited for it to come up. She should have known: there was a holographic image of Hannah-Ben Shurlamp standing there on the tabletop, dressed in white with hints of raven peeking through here and there ready to assist her in performing her queries.

She looked up the words and soon had a list:

abnojax: An idiomatic term with no direct translation in the League common. It meant, most literally "amnesia", but what it implied was to simply have the ability to quickly forget about a setback and continue on. To be persistent, no matter what.

Hmm, Stenibelle had to admit, that would be a handy one to have.

crixamp: (N)—determination.

ventross: (N)—ferocity.

verapone: (N)—resourcefulness

fenve: (N)—pugnaciousness

So, here they were, arcane bolabungs covering a whole shortlist of all the virtues Hannah-Ben Shurlamp felt she was sorely lacking in; and again, Shurlamp's assessment appeared to be rather correct.

She certainly wasn't overly resourceful, fierce or pugnacious. She had allowed Lt. Gwendolyn of Prentiss to board her ship without so much as a protesting whimper, without a cross word uttered in reprisal. Private Taara had wanted her to stand up to Gwendolyn, to fight her if need be.

Truth be told, Stenibelle was frightened of the imposing Gwendolyn and she meekly did as she was told right in front of A-Ram and Taara. She didn't say two words to her as she strode onto her bridge to take command. She couldn't devine any way to get her stricken, scuttled ship away from Gwendolyn. What could she have done? There was no way she could have gotten out of it.

"I thought you had something!" Taara spat as she was led off in irons to face Marine punishment for being AWOL.

And, Stenibelle certainly didn't have amnesia; she remembered it all and felt it just as much. Lt. Gwendolyn's haughty behavior certainly didn't help matters. She was far from a silent, professional Fleet officer. She lectured Stenibelle and went out of her way to humiliate her, making Stenibelle's blood boil to that very day, yet she couldn't muster the nerve to stand and fight back. Even in retrospect she couldn't think of an alternate course of action or think up something witty to say to Lt. Gwendolyn. Her wit failed her into submissive silence, even in her own head.

So now, perhaps with these bolabungs, she might be able to alter circumstances to her liking. Perhaps, all "Bunged Up" she could have gotten away from Gwendolyn and not been incarcerated.

A-Ram and Taara standing there, watching her get frog marched out of the dead bridge in irons.

The humiliation, the guilt.

She felt her stomach turn and her spirits sag. That was seven months ago, but the memory was just as crushing now as it was then.

Now, sitting in front of her was instant courage, instant resourcefulness, instant ferocity. The person these bolabungs could turn her into . . . imagine.

But, she had to be careful. These weren't wormwood trifles slathered in man-scent to stoke the libido, these were bolabungs of the highest quality and power meant to alter her very personality and they could harm her if worn improperly; addiction could be an issue. She also wondered at the great black mark of dishonor her House would suffer should she be caught. She had to be careful and limit their use.

She found some paper and quickly drew up a log book, marking the dates and times of their use, building in intervals of rest when she would remove them. She would stay on the safe side, wearing the bolabungs for no longer than three hours at a time, and even less so when wearing all of them at once. If she stuck to the log she should be fine.

She crawled into bed and dimmed the lights, listening to the mannequins move about the room. In the morning, she would try the bolabungs on and note it in her log.

She closed her eyes and dreamed of her House, Belmont Manor on the hill by the sea. How she wished she could go home and see her sisters.

Morning soon came. The mannequins gently nudged her awake. *"Ottoman John, Esa, will be fetching you at 10 bells,"* one said in a musical voice. *"Your journey to Planet Fall begins promptly at 11 bells. Breakfast will be served you aboard the* Hoban Night.*"*

She clambered out of bed and had a refreshing shower. Drying and donning her knickers, she seated herself at the boudoir and annotated in her logbook.

8 Bells, tested bolabungs for fifteen minutes.

It was time to give them a try, to see if they made her feel sick or addled her constitution. Then she would remove them after fifteen minutes and continue dressing. Stenibelle opened the chest and took the bolabungs, all five of them, and put them on, situating her mass of black hair over their leather cords. The charms clinked together and settled at her breast.

The effect was immediate. It was a revelation.

She had thought the bolabungs would make her feel sick, on the contrary, she felt strong. She felt invincible. The sickening feeling of the events of seven months ago was suddenly gone, suddenly had no meaning.

Gone was the indecision. Gone was the pain.

So she went into space and failed? So what? So some of her sisters were embarrassed by the incident? What were they doing to preserve the House? Nothing!

So she was handcuffed and made sport of—she was wronged by an uncaring Fleet and an oaf of a Lt.

Gwendolyn, Lady of Prentiss . . .

Stenibelle's blood boiled. How dare she set foot aboard *her* ship that she paid for and how dare she presume to lecture her!

I should have had you on the ground, screaming for mercy! Taara was right, I should have knocked your teeth out!

Before she knew what was happening, Stenibelle had her fist through the mirror, the broken shards of silvered glass raining down all over. Wheeled mannequins came in a hurry to attend to the broken glass. She went into the bathroom and washed her bleeding hand. Small cuts, nothing to be concerned over.

All "Bunged up" and finally free of the haunting memories of the past, she was eager to leave the confined environs of Hannah-Ben Shurlamp's manor; Planet Fall awaited. The place ought to be a veritable paradise for her full of dark alleys and unsavory types to test out the new, ruthless, uncaring Stenibelle. Everything she had done previously was for her House, for Belmont-South Tyrol, for her father and her sisters. Now, it was time to do for herself, to build her own fortune and reputation, to not care about her heritage or Belmont Manor that she had dreamed of so fondly the night before. Perhaps Hannah-Ben Shurlamp would be proud of what she had created.

She got out her HRN and men's clothes and sorted through all of her things. From the hidden interior of the HRN, came an assortment of items the officials at Hagthorpe had never found. She waved her hand and there was her MARZABLE dagger, black and ornate, ready for use. She moved her hands again and it was gone.

Another shake and she had six nested daggers between her fingers gleaming and ready to kill. A final shake and they were gone.

Digging further in the hidden contents of her coat were a number of Holystones of various colors, a few silvery devices designed to detect and counter the arcane, and a Grenville 40 pistol that she used in place of her

NTHs, which didn't function.

As with everything, Professor Shurlamp seemed to know that Stenibelle made use of a Grenville 40, as there was a box of ammunition for it conspicuously placed in the closet. She loaded up and made the box vanish.

She packed everything back up, dressed and was ready to go. On the bell, Ottoman John knocked on her door. "I see you are kitted out in your usual attire," he said. "Though you are dressed as a man, you are still a very attractive lady."

Stenibelle took the compliment and responded. "You have no chance, sir," she said.

Ottoman absorbed that. "I see. The *Hoban Night* shall be your transport to Planet Fall, all expenses paid and First Class booking, of course. It will shortly be in position and we shall upload you to it with all speed. Once there you will be served breakfast. However, before that happens, we have one final stop to make. Please, if you would kindly accompany me."

"How about the Professor? Will she see me off?" Stenibelle asked.

"No, my lady."

They exited the room, Stenibelle's logbook sitting on the boudoir, forgotten.

✳　✳　✳　✳　✳

Ottoman John led her down several corridors until they arrived at a baroque door. He produced a set of keys and opened it. "After you," he said, bowing.

Stenibelle entered the room and was immediately taken aback. Inside was a long table covered with oblong boxes. The boxes were all open, with the lid to each box fitted underneath like a shoe box. Festive, brightly colored tissue paper blossomed from each box. Stenibelle took a glance. Within each open box, wreathed in pastel paper, was a VUNKULA, the LosCapricos weapon of House Grenville.

Ottoman John spoke as Stenibelle took in the staggering wealth that was presented before her, for VUNKULAs were costly in the extreme: "Professor Shurlamp knows of your proficiency with this weapon, and as she is invested in your success, she bades you take one of your choice."

Stenibelle feasted her eyes on the dormant hints of golden links and glint of jewels peeking out of the paper awaiting discovery. "These are priceless."

"Of course they are. This is a gift from your generous benefactor."

She stepped down the line, perusing the boxes, Stenibelle saw VUNKULAs of all shapes and sizes: big ones, small ones, gilded ones, cruel war-like examples and many with multiple tails. The VUNKULA was a sturdy belt that went around the waist. Attached to the center of the belt was a metal tail made of forged interlocking links. They averaged anywhere from three to eight feet long at full stretch and were tipped with a variety of barbs, hooks, points, arrows and other club-like constructions, each VUNKULA was unique. The interior of the belt was lined with fragments of the Mindstone, thus, when worn, a skilled practitioner could bring the tail portion to life, moving like a prehensile monkey's tail. The most common usage of the weapon was to keep it hidden within one's clothing. When needed, it could be dipped into a variety of substances kept in hidden pockets and then strike in the blink of an eye, inflicting a deadly blow. A proper VUNKULA attack was a lightning strike, the victim never seeing it come or go.

"Lord Geyron of Grenville, a former suitor of mine, once gave me a VUNKULA for my birthday, and he taught me to use it well," she said. "It was just a little one."

"He must have thought much of you to offer such a gift."

"You are the most beautiful woman I have ever seen, Bel."

"He liked me well-enough."

The gift was gone—it had helped pay for her trial. Lord Geyron was gone too, her scandal had been too much for a stately Grenville to bear.

"Your letters have all been returned, Bel." Virginia told her.

"Professor Shurlamp knows all about it," Ottoman John said. "Select any of your choosing, but please make haste, we must to the *Hoban Night* within the hour."

It was like standing in a butcher's shop perusing all the choice cuts of meat, her mouth watering at the gorgeous selections. Stenibelle ignored the smaller, daintier ones of light metals and crusted with decorative jewels clearly made for ladies and for stabbing necks, focusing instead on the bigger, brutish, more war-like ones for men made to break necks. She wanted one that was big enough for her to attack at a distance, to use it like a third fist. She found what she was looking for. In a box bursting with teal paper was a pugnacious one made of cockspur, a very hard and durable metal from Hoban. She pulled it out of the box, it was tipped with a Hoban Battle Club, a rudimentary, three-fingered hand that could open and close into a fist. Very useful. She had found the perfect one.

"I think that one might be too big for you, my lady," Ottoman John said.

"Rubbish. It's perfect," she replied. Stenibelle removed her sash and strapped the belt on. As it settled, she felt the tail come under her control, ready for her command. As Ottoman John had said, it was too long for her small stature, the club dragging on the floor. She concentrated and recalled Lord Geyron patiently teaching her its use. The tail shuddered and then lifted from the floor and came to her eye level. The hand at the end of the tail turned, the fingers opened and closed. She noticed a small glyph sticking out of Ottoman John's coat pocket. She extended the tail in his direction and gently plucked the glyph from his pocket, showed it to him, and then offered it back.

"Very precise control, Lady Stenibelle. I am impressed," he said, taking his glyph.

She coiled the tail up and it vanished under the folds of her HRN. She covered the VUNKULA's belt with her green sash, replaced her NTH's and was ready to go. "Shall we?" she said, and they retired from the room. "I'm starving. I wish to be served something raw."

She was led out to the primordial commotion of the yard and into a waiting ripcar. Soon, she was in her room aboard the *Hoban Night*, on her way to Planet Fall, seething to get started.

4—Planet Fall

Stenibelle's eyes smoldered as she sat at the cafe under the rapid orange sky.

It's her . . .

Two days prior, Stenibelle had taken the long trip from Kana across open space past the Corvus-Arch and arrived at Hoffman Plate, Planet Fall. A gas giant rich in trace elements, Planet Fall was home to three man-made continents floating in the upper atmosphere. Hoffman Plate was one of them, drifting in the clouds in the withering gravity. There, in the towering buildings and dark streets vibrating with counter-gravity, dreams of fortune and building one's self into something greater came into conflict with the reality of wealth and the reality of social mobility. On Hoffman Plate, the Sisters were seldom seen, the Great Houses held diminished sway and the glories of the past meant nothing compared to the naked steel of the here and now.

Such spirit fit with the new Stenibelle and she spilled out onto the streets like a pool of oil waiting to catch fire. She settled into her rented, all-expenses paid room at an inn near the ship docks and up-sized it, taking all the inn had to offer, eating the most expensive foods, ordering spirits and other Planet Fall delights, all on Professor Hannah-Ben Shurlamp's dime. And there she waited, restless, getting a feel for the city and the sickening tug of Planet Fall far below.

She was ready for anything as she scanned the skies from her centrally-located terrace and from the cafes on the street. Setting up a small lab in her room, she set to work restocking her supply of Holystones, astral plane detectors and other arcane devices. She also spent a day or so conjuring up something she felt could be her "Ace in the Hole" . . . Black Maidens.

Gaunt and fairly benign spirits of the elemental plane of air, the Maidens were one of her deceased mother's favorites. With great skill, and a bit of peril thrown in, the Black Maidens could be summoned from the plane of air and be bound to a certain area indefinitely. She could set them after a person just by scent alone or by their blood, and if they caught the person, they would teleport them right back to where they were initially summoned. Stenibelle's mother, Lady Jubilee, once used the Black Maidens to follow and summon herself and her sisters back to Belmont Manor, their maddening ability to locate one when least expected was utterly frustrating. She knew, firsthand, how difficult it was to get away from a pursuing Black Maiden when mother sent them.

She needed a quiet, out-of-the way, room that she could use not only as a place to summon the Black Maidens, but to also use as a sort of arcane fortress and prison for those she might capture with them. It had to be good-sized, sturdy and quiet.

Combing the environs in and around the docks, she found a decent-sized building down the street that appeared to be abandoned. Using her MARZABLE daggers to scale the walls like an invisible gecko and her VUNKULA gripping the wall for added support, she found a perfect space several floors up and slithered in through the window. Having a third hand was indispensable. Apparently a former warehouse space of some sort, it was open and had only a single door leading down to the floors below. The door was welded shut and the interior was stark, made of bare metal and concrete. She wrenched the door open with her VUNKULA and locked it with a cypher-lock paid for by Hannah-Ben Shurlamp. It was perfect. There, she set up her tripod, pots and other arcane necessities needed to summon Black Maidens. Once ready, she lit a fire under the tripod and burned the various herbs and tinctures needed for the summoning. In the past, she'd always been a little fearful of summoning Black Maidens. It was very easy to have the summoning go wrong and get something much worse than a Black Maiden. Stenibelle, while training with her mother, accidentally summoned a Soul Devourer once and had been frightened half to death before Mother got rid of it. She'd been hesitant to summon them ever since, the leering Soul Devourer put a shudder in her.

However, with the Bolabungs around her neck and her new VUNKULA ready to sting, she had no hesitation. She spoke the strange words her mother had taught her and summoned dozens of them. They floated about the room in a black-veiled cloud, orbiting, silently awaiting their turn to return to their airy home, and here they would stay until released. She then created dozens of scented brown Holystones. Black Maidens were very much creatures of smell, and when the scented oils within the Brown Holystones were released, a Maiden would come and instantly teleport whomever carried the scent right back to this room, and then the Maiden would be released to return to her home. Her mother had a room in Belmont Manor always full of Black Maidens and Stenibelle herself had been teleported to it many times in the past. Late for dinner, out with an unacceptable male companion, out doing unlady-like things and BAMF!! She would be right back home again to face mother's wrath.

In that abandoned room surrounded by the gaunt, airy Maidens, Stenibelle readied herself for battle. She had her MARZABLE dagger ready to go. With it, one dagger could become as many as she needed and she could never be disarmed. She often created six of them at a time nested between her fingers. She also ground up a number of powders and salves: poisons, sedatives, truth-tellers, mind-clouders and so on. She placed them into select pockets within her HRN. Now, she could select whatever she needed as the situation required and dip in with the tip of her VUNKULA, ready to administer a lightning blow like a scorpion's sting.

Though she usually carried her NTH's in her sash, she couldn't use them. They could not be fired by a woman. Bunged-Up into a more practical frame of mind, she left them in their case at the inn. She replaced them in her sash with something more practical: her silver Grenville 40 pistol and a Hertamer variable select heat gun that she'd bought in a Ready Shop down the street. She then tricked the floor of her "Black Maiden" room with purple Holystones balanced on delicate stands set to release a potent knock-out gas. If anybody happened to show up in the room, they would most likely cause a Holystone to fall from the stands, thus releasing the gas and rendering them unconscious. Stenibelle herself had built up an immunity to the gas during her years of training.

✳   ✳   ✳   ✳   ✳

And she used her little dungeon quite a bit in the idle time waiting for the *George Parr* to arrive. She had taken to petty robbery. Seeing people passing through the docks, seeing them walking about alone off of newly-arrived ships wearing interesting rings, jewelry and other assorted trinkets, some a bit sickened and disoriented from the anti-gravity, Stenibelle brazenly stalked and fell on them like a common thief, creeping up on them, fooling them with batted eyes and pretty smiles, and then getting them with the brown Holystone, watching the Maiden appear and then seeing them vanish. Returning to her dungeon at the end of the street, she found her victims unconscious on the floor near cracked-open purple Holystones. Stealing what she wanted, Stenibelle cast them out to the alley where they would eventually wake up.

Welcome to Planet Fall.

*   *   *   *   *

She didn't have things completely her own way, though. Stenibelle was soon accosted by a woman, dressed in her Planet Fall worst, painted, leggy, pierced and red-eyed. It was an Eryne, one of those fanatical prostitutes all jumped-up on the Weed. She'd heard of them before, they were supposedly mean, unruly and nothing to trifle with. They were personages the old Stenibelle would have shrunk from, would have crossed the street to avoid.

"You're peddling your little ass on the wrong street, darlin'," the Eryne said in a thick Planet Fall accent. "I seen you skulking about."

The new, Bunged-Up Stenibelle, however, would not be intimidated. She bellied up to the woman, got into a shouting match with her and they ended up in the alley. Stenibelle had never been in a street fight in her life, had never even come close, yet, there she was in a full-on fist-swinging, clothes-tearing, hair-pulling brawl with an Eryne prostitute over, of all things, whoring turf on Planet Fall. She was actually enjoying it, the contact, the noise, hearing the horrid woman grunt and groan with every blow, listening to the fabric of her clothing rip between her fingers and utter oaths and curses as she, not Stenibelle, slowly wore down. Stenibelle could have VUNKULAed her, could have stabbed or shot her, but instead contented herself with a mere beating. She blackened both her eyes, knocked out a few teeth and then, almost mercifully, applied the Brown Holystone.

The Black Maiden appeared and the battered prostitute vanished.

Later that evening, Stenibelle passed through the cypher-locked door and found the woman in the dungeon along with a few other victims, face down and unconscious, the room stinking of purple Holystone gas. Stenibelle robbed her and the others blind and put them all out in the alley on top of the trash.

The next day, Stenibelle was accosted yet again as she sat at an outdoor cafe drinking a coffee, this time by the whore's master.

"Inga! Inga!" he called out from the roof of a nearby building, calling her some sort of bad Planet Fall name. Several people sitting nearby stood and took their leave, leaving Stenibelle to her apparent fate. She calmly drank her coffee and watched as the man and two garish whores dropped down, the three of them wearing those odd flying suits popular on Planet Fall, their clothes taking on a stilted, bat-like appearance as they flew.

They came down and approached. The man, a seedy Planet Fall Whore-Master, stood there in butternut, backed up by his two whores in unsightly whoring gowns, all spoiling for a fight, all spoiling for revenge.

"So, Inga," the dirty, butternut-dressed man said, "think you to cut into my profits, do you? My ladies work these streets, all the way to the docks, and if you think I am going to allow you to run a trade on my time, you're sorely mistaken. Get up!"

One of the whores reared back and pounded a knife dripping with cheap poison into the tabletop. A situation like this would have once been the stuff of her nightmares, now, she sat there in grim excitement. What to use on these people, what to do to them? Her mind boggled on it for a moment.

Covertly within the folds of her HRN, she slid the battle club of her VUNKULA into a pocket full of fine powder. It was time.

The two armed whores came at her, slobbering for a fight.

FHATOOM!

FHATOOM!

The VUNKULA shot out twice, pricking the whores each in the neck, getting them with sleeping powder and they went down without a hitch, their poisoned knives clattering to the street. The butternut Whore-Master was open-mouth shocked seeing his rough and ready girls eliminated so quickly, and, though he'd been looking right at them, the VUNKULA attack was so swift and precise, he had no idea what had happened. One moment they were up, the next they were down. He drew a Hit 6 Fraglock pistol from his filthy coat.

BAM!

This time she balled the VUNKULA's battle club into a fist and crossed his face, breaking his jaw with ease.

BAM!

She slammed him in the other direction with devastating force and he went down, eyes watering, jaw ajar, dropping his pistol.

That fast the fight was over. Stenibelle seated herself and resumed drinking her coffee. The Whore-Master crawled away leaving his girls on the street.

She anticipated no further troubles. Thus armed and tricked out and having established her "turf" by force of arms, she waited for the *George Parr* to arrive.

There was no posted information on when it would arrive as the Fleet did not share such things openly, however, "Bunged Up" with a new persistence and resourcefulness, Stenibelle wasn't going to let that stop her. She made friends with the unsavory locals, the dark men rolling back and forth near the docks, the Erynes fretting for their livelihood, but giving her space. Using her feminine guile in a seductive and ferocious manner, she quickly had several men under her sway. One man, with ties to the Astro-Traders, told her that The *George Parr* was orbiting Kama at the moment. The word was she was soon to set out for Planet Fall.

Some of the men told her the *George Parr* was hiring K-Lister crew out of Onaris. The inside word was that the *George Parr* was doing something illegal, possibly running contraband to the Xaphans.

The men's price for their help was the usual when dealing with a pretty young woman. They wanted sex. When she felt inclined, she offered it to them, other times she incapacitated them with a kiss in the neck from her VUNKULA and left them passed out in her chamber of horrors. Before taking her leave, she would empty their pockets and rob them blind, her dungeon filling with loose odds and ends from her victims: money of various currencies, neck ties, brooches, pins, Cred Sticks from Bazz, papers, handkerchiefs, time pieces, hats, attaché cases, holo-pads, latch keys, small arms and on and on. She even had stolen somebody's shoes.

✳   ✳   ✳   ✳   ✳

Two days later standing on her rented terrace, she watched the long, straight line of the *George Parr* come down through the banded clouds above the containment dome and make berth at the docks.

Her Ceril Cone information from Professor Shurlamp barged into her head: *Infiltrate the* George Parr. *Get the stellar location of Cammara. All other considerations secondary.*

But she was having so much fun abducting and stealing and fighting. Stenibelle put on her HRN and hat and made her way down to the dock. She couldn't help herself, she abducted two more lone passersby along the way. It was so easy.

There it was at last, her quarry: the *George Parr*, lashed to the dock, white as snow, ten stories tall. The main gangway was open and people in Fleet uniforms were coming and going at a busy rate. As she looked at the people coming out of the ship, she was suddenly engulfed with information.

That man there—he's Gregory de Lopol of Bazz, cook's mate. The woman with the pad, she's Crewman Endry of Chole, logistical wing.

Professor Shurlamp's Ceril-Cone. She must have downloaded the entire known complement of the *George Parr's* crew into her brain. That would be a big help going forward.

Trying to blend in, she made her way to the gangway and attempted to enter the ship.

A Marine standing guard tipped his hat and stopped her. "Good day, madam. Well met," he said. "Have you business aboard the ship this afternoon?"

"I am here to see Captain Duval."

The Marine checked a pocket terminal. "I'm sorry, madam, I do not see any visitors scheduled for today, which isn't surprising as we've only just arrived. I'm sorry for any confusion, however, I cannot grant you access to the ship. Please contact Fleetcom and ask to speak to Civilian Affairs to have this matter addressed and corrected."

Stenibelle entertained the passing thought of cracking him on the forehead with a Brown Holystone and sending him via Maiden to her dungeon. She'd love to steal that red Marine coat of his. But instead she thanked him and walked away. When she was out of sight, she faded into the shadows and returned, this time walking right past the guard without being detected. She stood up on the ends of her feet and gave him a light kiss on the cheek. The Marine brushed his hand across his face, oblivious.

Unobserved, Stenibelle was about to enter the *George Parr* when she saw something that stopped her in her tracks.

Berthed several blocks away was a small scouting ship, only recently arrived. The ship was just in and was "gassing" in steamy plumes to equalize the internal pressure. Mooring beams were inching the ship into its final position and the gangway was just now being extended.

Bunged Up and sharp-eyed, Stenibelle saw the name of the scout ship:

Demophalon John.

That was the bloody scouting ship that intercepted her in space, docked and cost Stenibelle her chair.

Forgetting about her mission, she dropped out of the shadows and made her way to the ship. She arrived at its moorings just in time for the gangway to be secured and the main hatch to be opened.

People began spilling out of the ship onto the dock.

Once, the memory of this ship, even the sound of its name caused her nothing but grief and humiliation.

But now . . .

She leaned back against the brick wall and watched the Fleet crew and various other persons filter off the ship, some engaging in business with the dock hands, others dispersing into the depths of the city.

Some of the men coming off the ship cast her an approving eye as they passed.

A tall, stern-looking woman in a Fleet uniform and long brown hair emerged from the hatch and came down the gangway. A scabbarded rapier swung at her hip. Stenibelle noticed how the Fleet crew and others got out of her way and generally avoided her as she passed. With her nose buried in a portable terminal, she moved onto the dock and turned left into the mass of city buildings of Hoffman Plate.

"Are you Lady Stenibelle of Belmont-South Tyrol?" she remembered.

She remembered the tall woman stepping aboard the *Seeker's* docking ring.

She remembered the stern, disapproving eye.

"You could at least have made this difficult."

It's her!! It's Lt. Gwendolyn!!

Her VUNKULA wreathed in its coils. Disgust and pent up anger filled her up and, quickly, Stenibelle followed, pushing through the crowd assembled on the docks.

Lt. Gwendolyn went several blocks into the city, walking as if pre-programmed, her nose buried in the terminal the whole time. She wasn't difficult to follow, she walked slowly without a care. She moved through the crowds completely disconnected from the masses around her, as if they didn't exist. After a fair amount of time had passed she absent-mindedly selected a street-side cafe and was shown to a table. Seated, served a coffee, she stirred the cup with a spoon as she continued to read from her terminal. She cast an absent-minded glance at a silver watch perched on her left wrist.

Without hesitating, Stenibelle came into the cafe, made her way to the lady's table and loudly seated herself. At last, Lt. Gwendolyn looked up from her reading, her expression a mixture of shock and anger.

"Hello, Lt. Gwendolyn," Stenibelle said with a flourish.

Gwendolyn stared at her for a moment, without recognition. Then: "Oh, it's you, from the *Seeker*, yes?"

"That's correct. Do you not choose to recall those from whom you steal?"

"Steal?" Gwendolyn sat back and pushed her terminal away. She was apparently struggling with the events that had occurred, trying to sort them out and recall them properly. "Oh yes—yes! Now I remember. Your pardon, aren't you supposed to be in prison?"

Stenibelle gave a wicked smile, showing her teeth. "I was released. I saw you walking off your ship and couldn't resist the urge to say 'hello'."

Gwendolyn regarded her for a moment and returned to stirring her coffee. "Yes, well. I did my duty and followed my orders. You don't have to be happy about the matter. I suggest you take advantage of this second opportunity you've somehow been granted and apply yourself to matters better suited to you."

Stenibelle placed her small hands on the tabletop and clawed at the tablecloth. "Matters better suited to me? And what might those be?"

"I'm certain I don't know."

"Sitting in a parlor, perhaps? Waiting for some man to come twirling by and sweeping me away? I have spent the last seven months in prison wondering what I'd say if I ever saw you again. I do believe that I hate you."

"Truly," Gwendolyn said. "Well, I do not hate you, Lady Belpre . . ."

"Belmont!" she yelled, slamming her fist on the tabletop. Gwendolyn raised her eyebrows for a moment and then returned her attention to her terminal.

"I will ask," Stenibelle said with a certain tautness in her voice, "what are your lingering impressions as you boarded my ship and cost me my command and my freedom? What stands out?"

"The matter has faded in my memory."

"Put your head into it. I'm certain it'll come back to you," Stenibelle growled, grinding her teeth.

Gwendolyn thought a moment. "If you like, I thought you were a little girl in waters well above your depth. I don't recall seeing any particular ingenuity, initiative or charisma on your part. Your motley crew, if I recall, seemed to have more drive and pluck than you did. You realize, of course, that you could have been responsible for their deaths—the *Seeker* was not habitable and I'm glad I put a stop to your misadventure before anybody got hurt. Finally, if I am tasked to be honest, I thought you looked scared. I pitied you, actually."

Stenibelle seethed. "I see. Would you care to accompany me to the alley, where we may discover once and for all who is to be pitied?"

Gwendolyn chuckled. "Oh please . . ."

Stenibelle erupted from her seat and seized Gwendolyn by the lapels. All eyes in the cafe turned to them. "Or right here, perhaps! I shall command your complete attention one way or the other!"

Keeping her composure, Gwendolyn slowly stood. As she rose to full height, she was nearly a foot taller than Stenibelle. "Unhand me, please. If you wish this, then so be it and perhaps then I'll be able to enjoy my dinner in peace."

Stenibelle let her go and they quickly made their way out of the cafe and into an adjacent alley. Several people attempted to follow them to watch, but a scathing look from Stenibelle put them back into their seats. The alley was a tad narrow, but, for the moment, was clear of people.

"Are you certain you wish this?" Gwendolyn asked removing her Fleet coat. "I truly do not wish to hurt you."

Stenibelle quickly flashed six MARZABLE daggers between her fingers and displayed them to Gwendolyn. "I'm certain."

Gwendolyn was nonplussed. "I'm not going to duel with you, Lady Belmont, I've my career to think of. If you wish to fight, then I shall be willing, however, I'll not engage in a duel. If you wish to register with the Sisters as is proper and await their approval, then I shall meet you for a duel, but not before."

Stenibelle waved her hands and the MARZABLE vanished. She then began removing her collection of rings and bracelets, all recently stolen, and made them vanish. She removed her HRN and set her Grenville 40 and her heat gun aside.

Gwendolyn had nothing but a demure silver watch on her wrist. It looked expensive. She took her watch off and placed it in the folds of her coat. She fussed about with it, changing its location several times. "I will ask that my watch be out-of-bounds. It is a cherished keepsake and

I do not wish it damaged."

"Your man give you that?"

Gwendolyn didn't reply. She seemed to have nothing and no one. There were no hangers-on, none of her crew present. It was possible she didn't have a friend anywhere in the League. That crazy woman Alesta had said that she (as a man) and this Gwendolyn person cared for each other—that she (he) stirred her heart. She had seen the photo of herself (himself) standing next to Gwendolyn. Her expression and demeanor didn't seem much different than now as she prepared for a fight, but in the picture it seemed like she had a place and was among those with whom she was comfortable; it seemed like she belonged.

Here, she belonged nowhere.

She clenched her fists. Her knuckles popped. As she waited to start, a tiny voice bubbled up from within.

What are you doing? Where is your heart? What have you become?

Her feelings were lost, Bunged-Up and buried beneath months of frustration and humiliation.

Remember when you prevented Lucile and Lyra from having a fight in the cruiser? And you got Lenta and Munni talking again after their Nether Day fall out?

You stop fights. You make peace. Your heart is your best asset. What have you become?

The word "addiction" popped into her head, the influence of the Bolabungs clear, the forgotten log book that she never used, yet she was caught up. She wanted nothing more than to lay her hands on this woman. Now, she felt nothing but rage and the need for revenge.

Gwendolyn moved her rapier aside and Stenibelle began the fight, swinging with an eager fist. Gwendolyn caught it and brought her down to the alley floor. She was doing some sort of grappling technique, trying to move Stenibelle's arm into a painful hyper-extended position. She was trying to quickly end this. Stenibelle wiggled her arm free and socked Gwendolyn across the jaw, connecting with a nice smack, sending her down to one knee. Gwendolyn tried to stand and Stenibelle hit her again and again. Too late Gwendolyn realized how hard Stenibelle was going to fight and couldn't recover.

Two more blows to the face and Gwendolyn spat out a bloody tooth. Enraged, she lashed out with a right hook that caught Stenibelle in the ribs. The blow was incredibly painful, but she wasn't to be stopped. Stenibelle pressed on, moving fast, not allowing Gwendolyn to square up and hit her properly. Blow after blow landed and Gwendolyn, mouth bloody, fell to the alley floor.

Triumphant, Stenibelle stood over her. Gods, but did that feel good! Stenibelle wrenched her up by the lapels, Gwendolyn's head lolled back, her mouth open and lined with blood.

"You awake?" she asked. No response, Gwendolyn was either unconscious or on the verge of it. Stenibelle leaned down and gave her a long kiss on the lips, imagining herself as a man and kissing her in such a fashion, dominating her, imposing her will and her strength. She was carried away in the moment, she felt powerful. She let Gwendolyn fall and licked the blood from her lips, savoring the taste.

"Oh, my dear, *how I love you* . . ." she growled in an ugly voice.

In the tussle, one of them had kicked her folded Fleet coat and her gleaming silvery watch lay on the alley floor.

Stenibelle wanted to hurt Gwendolyn and keep on hurting her. She stomped on it with the heel of her boot. Nothing happened, the watch appeared to be quite tough. She stomped on it again and again. The crystal cracked and the hands stopped moving. She was still not done torturing her. She waved her bloodied hand and produced a brown Holystone. She broke it open on Gwendolyn's sturdy forehead as if she were cracking an egg. A Black Maiden appeared a moment later and whisked Gwendolyn away, to the dungeon down the street she had prepared.

Thoroughly satisfied, she put her coat and other accessories back on. She pocketed the broken watch as a memento of this victory and returned to the cafe. She sat down at Gwendolyn's table and ordered dinner. There were a few Fleet personnel sitting at the cafe, possibly members of Gwendolyn's crew. None of them seemed concerned about her absence or checked the alley to see if she needed assistance. None of them seemed to care.

Gwendolyn's coffee and terminal sat there on the table, cold and forgotten.

5—A-Ram and Alesta Return

When Stenibelle returned to her room, she was somewhat surprised to discover her room was not empty.

Sitting inside were Lord A-Ram and Lady Alesta.

Alesta did not look happy. She sat forward in her chair, shoeless, her traveling boots removed and placed neatly in a corner.

"Well hello," Stenibelle said, removing her HRN. "I figured I'd be seeing the pair of you again, just not this soon."

Alesta didn't mince words. "Just what are you playing at?" she said in a strained voice.

Stenibelle sat down and poured herself a drink. "Sorry. Not certain I know what you're talking about."

"Gwendolyn! You could have killed her today!"

"Oh that. I was simply exercising my right to a little revenge." Stenibelle savored the memory of Gwendolyn face down in the alley, her watch cracking underfoot. She savored the memory of kissing her bloody mouth. "How is it you saw that? We were alone in the alley."

"We see everything, Bel. We watched you attack Gwen in the alley. And we've seen everything else as well. Kidnapping? Robbery? Random thuggery? How could you?"

Stenibelle curled her lip. "And what of it?"

A-Ram spoke up. "Bel, we think you're becoming addicted to those Bolabungs you're wearing. We headed back here as quickly as we could to help you out."

"I see. And where were you? Let me guess? Out gallivanting across the universes, assisting other, male versions of me? Is that right?"

"That's right."

"Did you two put that quaint picture in my coat?"

"We did," A-Ram said. "It was my idea. We thought it might help jog your memory or something."

Stenibelle pulled Gwendolyn's watch out of her pocket. "That picture is meaningless, and probably a fake."

"It is not, and you know it," A-Ram said. "Listen, this will come as a surprise to you, but, where we come from, you and Gwendolyn are very close. You love her in fact. She is to be your countess."

Stenibelle scoffed. "I cannot say much for my taste in women then, can I?"

"Your connection with Gwen spans the universes. Your souls are connected. I'd hoped that picture might stir those feelings within you."

"Oh, it stirred something, alright. Gwendolyn of Prentiss is a Shocktyte bitch and I am going to enjoy making her suffer. She took everything from me."

"She was doing her job," Alesta said.

"Perhaps she should get a different job. I bloodied her face today and broke her watch and enjoyed every moment of it. I don't believe I'm done with her just yet." Stenibelle gazed at the watch with cruel delight.

"That watch is a precious gift to Gwen! You gave it to her!" Alesta was shouting.

"Did I? Well, perhaps she can have it melted down for a paperweight."

"Bel!" Alesta yelled standing up. "Listen to yourself. That is not you talking. It's those damned Bolabungs you're wearing. They are getting into your mind, making you into something that you're not. We have freed Gwendolyn from your little prison, by the by—yes, we know all about your purple Holystone knock out gas and took precautions. She is safe and sound aboard her ship and has no idea of what you were planning on doing. Now, as a friend, because you are a person Rammy and I both cherish, I am going to kindly ask you to remove those bolabungs and give them to me. Give them to me now, and the watch as well." Alesta held out her hand.

Stenibelle scoffed. "You two are strangers to me. You say you know me, well I do not know you, and, for that matter, I don't know if I even like you or not! These bolabungs are a revelation. And this watch is a trophy dedicated to the new me. With these, there is nothing I can't do, nothing I can't accomplish! These bolabungs are going to build me a fortune. Why in the name of Creation would I want to be rid of them?"

"Because they are turning you bad, Bel!" Alesta said. "We know you have cause to be angry with Gwen. We know she was rather hateful to you; however, that does not give you the right to enslave her, to hold her in chains and torture her, to break things that are dear to her. The bolabungs are stripping you of your reason and your humanity! They are turning you into a thief and a selfish, hateful woman. Now, give them to me before it's too late! I'll not ask again!"

Stenibelle stood up and walked a few paces toward Alesta. She pushed her bosom out, proudly displaying the five colorful bolabungs hanging at her throat. "Then why don't you come and get them, if you can. Apparently, you saw what I did to that fool Gwendolyn, so what could you possibly . . ."

Before Stenibelle knew what was happening, Alesta sprang with surprising speed, grabbed her by the arm, threw her through the air and had her down on the floor, her soft but undeniably firm foot squarely planted on Stenibelle's throat. The watch flew from her hand and landed on the carpeting.

And then the bolabungs came away and her world faded into a prismatic spray.

✳   ✳   ✳   ✳   ✳

Stenibelle awoke, as from a fevered dream. She appeared to be in bed, floating atop the stormy seas of sanity boiling with disconnected memories and drifting voices.

She heard talking, wrapped in vivid color.

"I didn't know you could fight like that, Bear-bear."

"I'm a Dare, Rammy—we all get taught to fight. It's not a skill I hope to have to make use of often."

"Actually, I found it rather stimulating."

"Really?"

Stenibelle tried to say a few words and something leaned over her in the colored dark. "You're having a fever, Bel. Your mind became accustomed to the bolabungs, and is reacting to their loss. I'm sorry I had to do that to you. We're both here with you and we're not going anywhere."

"I'm . . . frightened . . ." Stenibelle's voice said, shaking.

"It's alright to be afraid, Bel."

Two figures got next to her in bed and held onto her trembling body. Like a buoy in a turbid sea, she clung to them and rode out the storm.

✳   ✳   ✳   ✳   ✳

She felt a soft kiss on her cheek. She reacted and licked her lips. Stenibelle replayed the scene in the alley in her mind. Standing over Lt. Gwendolyn, her mouth bloody. Savagely kissing her on the mouth in anger. The power she felt.

The anger was gone.

A moist pair of lips met hers and then fell away.

She opened her eyes. Ruddy morning light filtered in through the windows. Stenibelle was in bed surrounded by damp towels and rubber bottles filled with cool water. Her body ached all over.

A thin woman with shoulder-length, braided hair stood leaning over her holding a scanner.

"Alesta, A-Ram, she's awake," the woman said calling over her shoulder.

Stenibelle focused on the woman. She was swarthy and rather thin, wearing a tight Hospitaler uniform. Her face was made up and she had green eyes. She was holding a small scanner, pointing it at her head. A flickering light came out of the back end of the scanner bathing her in a reddish haze.

A-Ram and Alesta came in. Alesta carried a small coffee service. "Morning Bel," she said in a cheery manner. "It's wonderful to see you up. How are you feeling?"

Stenibelle's head was a wrung-out, sweaty mess. "My head hurts. Feel sick."

"That's normal," the Hospitaler said. "Bolabungs, especially the more complicated ones, have a persistent tendency to leech neurotransmitters from your brain. You're lucky. Your friends here went a long way in saving your life. You were quickly growing a terminal dependency."

"Who are you?" she asked.

The Hospitaler put her scanner away. "Morgan-Jeterix, Lady of Thompson."

"Do I know you?"

She gave a short laugh. "I just kissed you on the lips, what do you think?"

Stenibelle didn't know what to make of that.

Alesta put the service down and poured a cup. "We went and got Morgan, Bel. We wanted to make sure you were ok."

"Got her?"

"Yes. Morgan's dead in this reality."

Morgan winced a little. "Yep, there's only one of me, and here I am. The fire got me." Morgan's eyes seemed to dance with greenish light. "Want to see me do a trick?" she asked. "You like being scared? Bet I can scare the daylights out of you."

"I've no doubt," Stenibelle said.

"Morgan, you promised to behave," A-Ram said.

"Oh, but just look at her. She's so cute. I could just . . . suck her dry right now."

Morgan-Jeterix carried an intensity about her that unsettled Stenibelle. Unlike the bloody kiss from Gwendolyn that made her feel powerful, her lips where Morgan had kissed her felt cold and lifeless.

"We needed a Hospitaler immediately, Bel. You were very far off the grip, so we went and got Morgan."

"What? I was what?" she asked.

"Sorry, it's a Dare term. We thought we were losing you. We needed Morgan's expertise to assist in your care."

"It's rather funny seeing you like this, Bel," Morgan said. "But, it is you—genetically you're the same, except for the saturation of female hormones in your tissues, your breasts, your child-bearing pelvis, your vagina and other associated female plumbing, and you're over a foot shorter."

Stenibelle pushed the covers back and sat up, holding her head. She was wearing a sweaty nightgown.

Morgan gave her the once over. "And, will you look at those cute little feet? My Creation."

Stenibelle felt bashful. "What? My feet?" Morgan reached out to grab her foot and Stenibelle quickly moved them both away.

"Ha! Looks like some things never change no matter what realm of reality one finds oneself in. You're just as square here as a woman as you are back there as a man."

"Bel, don't mind Morgan—she has a novel sense of humor, and, she promised to behave. Haven't you, Morgan?" A-Ram said.

"Yeah, yeah. You have all the things I gave to you, yes? That's important, because you never know when I might go 'pop'."

"Right here," A-Ram said patting his coat.

Alesta offered Stenibelle a cup of coffee, which she accepted.

"So, I have a question. The three of you are from another universe or plane of reality, or whatever, is that right?"

"That's right, Bel," A-Ram said. "Think of it like this. There are an infinite number of universes, but we are concerned with only eight of them. There is an arcane device called the Anatameter out there that has pulled these eight universes together and tangled them up. Our mission is to assist you in untangling it. So, there are eight universes caught up in this mess, each a little different from the next, with Universes 1 and 8 being quite a bit different from each other. Me, Alesta and Morgan here come from Universe 1, ok? That's our home, that's where we belong. You come from Universe 3. So, right now, there are two of me in this universe. There's the A-Ram who's supposed to be here in Universe 3, the guy who flew with you on the *Seeker,* and then there's me. I'm a *Wvulgrom,* a visitor—I don't belong here, I belong in Universe 1, so does

Alesta. I'm here via arcane methods and won't be staying long. The other A-Ram is probably on Kana right now, back at the Fleet. It's the same with Alesta, she's out there somewhere too. There's only one Morgan, so she's the only one of herself."

"But how? How does that work?"

"Don't know. There's a lot of technology involved, it's all pretty complicated and we don't really understand how it works. We just go where we're told. We go here, we go there, we go where you need us. We also can't stay here forever, but in the short term no damage is done. We're here to guide you and the other versions of yourself. Once everything's fixed, we go back to where we belong and that's that."

She took a few sips of her coffee. "You seem to have great knowledge and understanding of this situation. Is it too much to hope that you know the information I seek for the Professor? Do you know the positioning of Cammara?" She was hopeful as she awaited their answer.

A-Ram frowned and shook his head. "No, Bel, we don't."

"Then I need to . . . need to resume my activities with the *George Parr* as soon as possible. I've information to collect."

"For the professor, Hannah-Ben Shurlamp, yes? I hate to tell you, Bel, but the *George Parr* is gone," Alesta said.

"Gone?"

"You've been flat on your back for the better part of a week," Morgan said.

She was alarmed. She wobbled out of bed and went to the terrace. Sure enough, the ship was gone, replaced at the dock by a seedy-looking Merchantman and a flock of dark Planet Fall birds.

She whirled around in frustration. "Now, what am I going to do? The Professor promised that she would provide me with information that could help preserve my House should I get her what she wanted. I thank you for your concern regarding my health, however I wish you would have allowed me to proceed unassisted. I've my House to think of. Should its preservation have cost me my sanity and my life, then so be it. I would have given them."

Morgan reached out and pinched her on the cheek. "Listen to her. Ohhh, you're just as dramatic as you are over there too."

Alesta put her cup aside and sat down on the bed. "I know you're disappointed, but we have an alternative plan. You're not alone. We're going to help you."

Stenibelle stood there. Her head ached. She couldn't think, couldn't make her mind work. "How? How can you help me?"

"Well, for one, the Professor cut you off the moment the *George Parr* blasted off and you weren't on it," A-Ram said.

"My room?" Stenibelle asked, somewhat alarmed. "I don't know if I have the money to pay the innkeeper at this time."

"You don't Bel. We paid the innkeeper."

Stenibelle blushed, unused to being a pauper. "Then I owe you some money."

"You don't owe us anything."

"I pay my debts, especially to my friends."

Alesta smiled. She beamed. "Bel, you consider us your friends?"

"Of course."

A-Ram joined in. "No worries, Bel. Our contact has given us quite a bit of information. Therefore, once you're ready, we can proceed."

Stenibelle rubbed her head. She felt slow-witted and dull. "Contact? What contact?"

Morgan gave a sly smile. "Go ahead, A-Ram, tell him, I mean her. Tell her."

Stenibelle awaited their answer as she tried to clear her head. A-Ram spoke. "Your wife, Bel, from another reality. She set us to this task. We couldn't refuse her."

"My wife?"

"A very kind, very enchanting woman. It is from her we get our information and our ability to cross the realms. She has vast technology at her disposal."

"Lt. Gwendolyn?"

"No!" Morgan said jumping in. She seemed flush with jealousy. "Not the *Merthig*."

A-Ram continued. "It's not Gwendolyn, Bel. She is a tall blonde-headed lady. Very stately, yet somewhat sad and full of care. She wears a flight suit, like a marine pilot, and carries a gun. That's what I remember most about her, the gun in its holster."

Stenibelle held her aching head. All this was too much for her. She lay back on the bed and closed her eyes. "What is her name?"

A-Ram and Alesta exchanged glances. "You know, she's never told us, and when in her presence it doesn't seem necessary to ask. She has a very mystical presence and she's an amazing woman, that is all we need to know."

Alesta spoke in her soothing voice, slowly, giving Stenibelle time to process. "There's more going on here than you could possibly know, Bel. It all has to do with a device that was stolen from you known as the Anatameter. You lost it, not here, but in Universe 1 where we come from. It wasn't your fault, but it is imperative that we re-claim it before the Nillists of Punts do. That is our overall task, and it will take us across Universes 1 to 8. As such, you and seven other aspects of yourself are caught up in it as well, and all eight of you have your specific roles to play in recovering it. That is the task we have been given, to guide you and the others as best we can."

"And, my wife with a gun and no name asked you to do this, for me?" she asked.

"She did."

"Then you are indeed true friends and I am sorry I didn't see it from the outset. So, tell me what I must do."

Alesta answered. "Yours is an important early step in our quest. In this reality, Universe 3, your goal is to discover Cammara. Once that is known, then the others may continue, so the Woman with the Gun has told us."

"Then I have failed. The information for discovering Cammara is on the *George Parr*."

"We shall take you there. We shall walk the Star's Road, Bel. We have permission," Alesta said.

"The Merian's Road? It doesn't exist."

"Yes it does. And with it, we can go anywhere we have laid eyes upon at a moment's notice. We can't do it from here though—there's too much power. We need a place where there are no power fields to disrupt it, someplace quiet and rural, far removed from the bustle of the city. We shall have to set out for Kana. Once there, we may walk our Road and we will send you to the *George Parr*."

"So then, my task is the same for you as it is for Professor Shurlamp, to get the stellar positioning for Cammara?"

"That's right. Once we know where Cammara is, we can look at it through a telescope and then travel there on the Merian's Road."

"I have been told that the Xaphan Rodrigo of Burgon has the information."

Morgan spoke up. "Your Professor has it wrong. She thinks Rodrigo of Burgon has the data and stealing it will be as easy as downloading it from him. That's not the case at all, is it Alesta?"

Alesta shook her head. "No. Rodrigo of Burgon doesn't know where Cammara is either, but he's seeking it for the same reasons we are, to get the Anatameter."

"And do what with it?"

"Put an end to the Universe."

A great bomb went off in Stenibelle's gut. "What? Is that possible?"

"It is. They've done it elsewhere, and it's not a pretty sight."

"Professor Shurlamp didn't think they could actually do such things."

"They can, and if they get to Cammara, they might just do it here as well. We have to get there first."

None of that made any sense to Stenibelle. She tried to stick to the concrete and easily understandable. "Then, where is the information?"

"The *Merten* has it," Morgan answered.

Alesta jumped back in. "Before you ask, Bel, there's one thing you need to understand. This quest spans the realities, spans the planes. It is an Extra-Planar quest, and, as such, it involves Extra-Planar entities. The *Merten* that Morgan refers to is an Extra-Planar entity."

Morgan stood and paced back and forth, full of nervous energy. "The *Merten* is my favorite," she said in an odd voice. "The *Merten* is a messenger of sorts, carrying the Universe's Mail. That's where the location of Cammara is kept, in the *Merten's* little head. Thing is, you usually have to kill the *Merten* to get it out. The information's not written down on a piece of paper, or scanned in a file, it's *inside* the *Merten*. Burn the *Merten*, bleed the *Merten*, listen to her dying breath. That's where you'll hear it."

"Who is this *Merten*?"

"Melazarr of Caroline," A-Ram answered.

Images flashed through her head. Professor Shurlamp's Ceril-Cone information bubbled up. "Melazarr of Caroline is a known associate of

Rodrigo of Burgon. She is his Tropist. She gives him pleasure."

"She is, she does, and she's never far from his side."

"And you're saying I have to kill this person?"

Morgan laughed. She seemed ferocious, intense, on the edge of delirium. "Who said that, Bel? Rodrigo of Burgon would have to kill her to get the information, but I don't think he's aware of her status. He thinks the information's going to come from a silly statue he lugs around, that if he feeds it enough Shadow tech it'll start talking and tell him what he needs to know. But, he's wrong, he's all wrong. It's his little Tropist giving him orgasms all day long that has it. When you show up, she'll give it to you."

"Why me?"

Morgan coiled up in sudden ferocity and opened and closed her fists. Though it may have been a trick of the light, her beautiful face became cracked and ugly. A-Ram reached into his coat and pulled out a small vial. He opened it and let Morgan take several sniffs. She seemed to calm a bit and lost her ferocity. Her face returned back to normal, if it had ever changed at all. A-Ram spoke. "Because you are also an Extra-Planar entity, Bel."

"Me?"

"You are a *Kaidar Gemain*. It's an old Cammarian term that means 'The One who is Everywhere.' You exist in every plane of reality, mostly as a man, here as a woman, and in others as an alien creature. That is very rare, most people do not exist in every plane, myself and Alesta certainly don't. Your status gives you a great deal of power, and Melazarz of Caroline will react to your presence and give you the information we need."

"Careful though," Morgan said. "*Mertens* die a lot. It's hard to keep a *Merten* alive."

Stenibelle sat up and tried to tame her wild black hair. "Well then, I'll do my best. Let's begin. Where are my clothes, please?"

"Bel, you need to rest another day or two," Alesta said.

"No, no! I'm ready to begin now. I've my House to think of."

Morgan walked away. "I'll get your clothes, you just sit there and relax, right cutie-pie."

Stenibelle was shocked as Morgan walked away. "I don't think I like that person," she said to Alesta.

"Bel, Morgan is a free spirit, and a tragic one too. She is also an Extra-Planer creature. She is a victim of circumstance and . . ." Alesta struggled for words. ". . . without proper chaperoning, she can be somewhat dangerous."

"Dangerous?"

"Rammy and I are here, and we will make certain she doesn't get out-of-control. You might as well know, where we come from, she loves you very much, and that loves carries with it a bit of danger. She was very angry you selected Gwen over her. Never fear. We are here to monitor the situation."

"When I what?? This is so confusing, hearing about things I've done, but I that I haven't done. And, if I'm being frank, if I were a man I cannot see myself picking either of them. Lt. Gwendolyn is a brooding giant of a woman, and this one is . . . well, I'm not certain what she is."

Morgan re-appeared holding Stenibelle's clothes. "I heard every word you said. I'll tell you what I am Bel. I, unlike you, am someone who's not afraid to follow her heart, no matter what cowardly bore or dreadful oaf it leads me to."

She took Stenibelle's pants and tossed them at her, forcing her to catch them. "I offered you something I'd not offered any before, not in centuries."

"Centuries?" Stenibelle asked.

"She's exaggerating," Alesta said.

She threw her shirt and her socks at her. "I am not. I was ready to commit myself to you alone, and look what I got for my devotion: ignored, cast aside. Humiliated."

"Yes, I know what that feels like quite well, thank you," Stenibelle said picking her clothes up.

Morgan held onto her coat. "And look. Look at this, you even have a teenie-tiny HRN coat too. How darling." Morgan's complexion seemed to take on a ghastly hue for a moment. "How darling," she said again in a slightly different voice.

"Where we come from, the Sisters did something to your HRN. It never shows any damage, it never even gets dirty. Is that the same here?" A-Ram asked.

Stenibelle put her hand out. "I have no idea. May I have my coat, please?"

Morgan held it up in the air, out of her reach. "You didn't say the magic word, Bel."

"I already said 'please'."

"That's not it," Morgan said.

"Then you have me. What is it?"

Morgan narrowed her eyes. "*Tempus Findal.*"

They checked out of the inn, A-Ram paying the bill, and made their way to the noisy docks. Several berths down, a white ship awaited them. As they got closer, Stenibelle saw the name of the ship and stopped dead in her tracks.

"The *Demphalon John*? This is our ship?"

"It is, Bel," Alesta said. "Rammy spoke to Lt. Gwendolyn and, as they are heading to Kana anyway, she agreed to allow us passage."

"How are we paying for the passage?"

"Never mind. It's paid."

Stenibelle recalled Gwendolyn face down in the alley. The bloody kiss. "She'll allow me to set foot aboard her ship?"

"It's already taken care of."

They went up the gangplank and checked in with the Marine guarding the entrance. He then escorted them into the interior of the ship where three small rooms awaited them. Stenibelle didn't see Lt. Gwendolyn along the way and was rather glad for it. She dreaded seeing her. She had no idea what she would say.

Soon the ship blasted away from Hoffman Plate.

6—THE DEMOPHALON JOHN

A day into their trip back to Kana, Alesta and Stenibelle practiced in her small room, all the furniture pushed aside giving them room to move. "So, do as I do," Alesta said. "This is a simple throw. You stand with your feet apart, your left foot in front of the right. Place your hands here and here, and then simply pull. I'll go flying over your shoulder."

Stenibelle did as Alesta advised and pulled on her smock, but nothing happened. Alesta was trying to teach her how to fight.

"I'm sorry," Stenibelle puffed. "I'm just not any good. You're a very patient teacher. May we take a break?"

"Certainly."

Stenibelle had warmed up to Alesta and A-Ram since the trip to Kana had begun. She now considered them dear friends.

"One thing that Lt. Gwendolyn said that's troubled me, Alesta," she said.

"What is it, Bel?"

"When I took the *Seeker* with A-Ram, I really had no idea what I was doing. Gwendolyn pointed out that I could have killed him due to my incompetence."

Alesta smiled. "But you didn't. There is a great person inside you. I watched you come and save us all. You got us food and a safe place to hide, and then you were ready to sacrifice yourself for complete strangers."

"That wasn't me, Alesta."

"Yes, it was. That same person is inside you. The reason I'm teaching you these techniques is not to demonstrate the basics of fighting, but to give you confidence, to believe in yourself. You can do so much, if you only gave yourself credit. You don't need a Bolabung to be great, Bel. Every day I see it more and more. The Bel I know as a man is a great man, and you are a great woman just waiting to shine through."

Stenibelle laughed. "Thanks."

The door opened and Morgan came through. Hands on hips, she surveyed the situation. "What are you doing?" she asked.

"I'm teaching Bel how to fight. Just some simple throws and so forth."

Morgan scoffed. "Look, if you want to know how to fight, you're not going to want to learn it from a Pilgrim of Merian. You have access to a real live Hospitaler—you know, 'Warrior/Healers', with an emphasis on the 'warrior' part."

Morgan flopped down onto the floor and pulled her boots off. "Come on, Bel, let me show you a few things."

Stenibelle didn't want to go out there with Morgan. She turned to Alesta.

"I think she's had enough for the day."

"Alesta, give us this room, please."

Alesta's expression darkened. She was skeptical. "I don't think that would be wise, Morgan, do you?"

Morgan offered a slightly wicked smile and licked her lips. "Why? What do you think I'm going to do, suck her dry or something? Think I'm going to freak out?"

Alesta wasn't going to budge. "You tell me."

Stenibelle nodded. If she couldn't face up to a slightly pushy and obviously eccentric Hospitaler, what could she do? "It's all right, Alesta."

Alesta sorted through her things and pulled out a small jug. She unstoppered it and held it out to Morgan. "Smell this first, please."

Morgan sighed and took a few whiffs of the open jug. "All right. All right. Thank you. I'm fine."

"What is that?" Stenibelle asked.

Morgan laughed. "Oh, just my 'Monster Juice'."

"And what is that?"

"I'll explain it to you later," Alesta said. "I'll be in the next room if you need me."

Alesta gathered her things and walked out. "Remember, Morgan, you promised," she said as she closed the door.

"What was all that about?" Stenibelle asked, a little put off.

"Nothing," Morgan said as she slowly approached her. "Those feet again," Morgan remarked looking down on them. "So cute."

"Must you antagonize me so?"

Morgan looked her up and down, taking in Stenibelle's curves. Her eyes sparkled with a greenish light. "I'm just stating the truth. So, here's your situation, you're in an alley and some lout comes out of nowhere spoiling for your cash or possibly your blood, what do you do?" Morgan advanced. She pushed Stenibelle hard on the shoulder. "What do you do?"

"I'd fade into the shadows and be on my way."

Morgan laughed. "Oh yeah, that little 'invisibility' trick you do? Go ahead. Turn invisible."

Stenibelle was a master at turning invisible, of fading into the shadows. Her mother had taught her and her sisters the skill, and Stenibelle was the best at it, with Lyra a close second. Her fade could fool sophisticated scanning systems and even arcane seeing eyes.

Morgan reached out and seized her by her shirt. She pulled her close and bared her teeth. "It doesn't work on me, Bel. I can see you plain as day. Now what? Now what are you going to do?"

Stenibelle had no idea what to do. She had no MARZABLE daggers, they were in the other room. She had removed her VUNKULA. She had nothing. She reached out, trying to grab hold of Morgan's arm and flip her as Alesta had just taught her. Morgan laughed and toyed with her. She bounced around, circling Stenibelle, batting her about the ears and face. "Come on, Bel, do something. I'm a crazed killer—I'm a monster—this is for keeps. Only one of us is walking away from this."

Frustrated, Stenibelle, went down and reached for Morgan's leg hoping to topple her over. She lifted it by the reverse of the knee, raising her thigh to level.

Morgan moved like a rabbit, wiggling free and taking Stenibelle down, wrapping up both her arms and her legs. Before she knew what was happening, they were in a tangle on the floor, Morgan's body intertwined with hers.

Her beaded braids came down into Stenibelle's face. "Now what are you going to do, Bel?"

She squirmed, trying to get free. No chance, Morgan had her down.

Morgan's green eyes blazed. "You and I could barely keep our hands off each other. You wanted me as much as I wanted you."

"That wasn't me. You speak of things that have never happened. Please let me go."

"Yeah, you're right. Nothing happened! You and your Gwendolyn . . ."

Tangled up with Morgan on the floor, Stenibelle felt the heat of her body. But, slowly, that heat faded, turning to dry, dank coldness that pulled the warmth from Stenibelle's body. Morgan brought her face in close, her breath freezing. "If I didn't need you so much, I'd show you some of the things I've learned over the centuries. I would claim you, Bel."

Stenibelle struggled, her body turning numb. "You're hurting me "

"So?"

"What do you need me for?"

Morgan rolled her over. "I need you to succeed. That's what I need. I need this whole bloody exercise to be a rousing success."

Light seemed to pour from Morgan's eyes and Stenibelle felt her heart freeze. Morgan had cast some sort of spell over her and she was unable to resist.

Morgan's hand, like a block of ice, slid down to the warm apex of Stenibelle's crotch and she parted her lips, moving in close. The touch was brutally cold, yet skilled and practiced and through the chill Stenibelle felt the first few vague notions of becoming aroused, of feeling the stabbing urge of delirium played by a dead hand on a withered page. Her heart pumped faster, her body stiffened and readied itself. "You feel that? You like that? I give pleasure and pain, all notes plucked from the same string. I could take you right now. Dead to rights, you would be mine, and it would be so easy." Stenibelle closed her eyes and bit her lip.

"Beg me to finish you off," Morgan said. "I know you're ready. A cold climax is something few people get to experience. Hot and sweaty is for the masses, for the pedestrian and people with no imagination. Cold and freezing mist, ah, now there's an experience. Everything tightening and turning blue. All your balloons ready to burst but they just won't go 'pop', will they? They fill and fill until you think you're going to pee your pants."

Stenibelle struggled.

Morgan clenched hard and that was it. Stenibelle groaned and clawed the floor. Her feet flexed and met with Morgan's. The release, the moving of fluids, her innards a mess. Stenibelle lay there in Morgan's frigid embrace, flaccid, half awake, half drifting away to a contented inner place floating above the river that had just been opened up within her. She stroked Stenibelle's tangle of black hair damp with drops of ice.

"What I just did to you, I once did to Kings, to Queens ages ago. Everyone wanted Morgan until they found out what Morgan really is and then they cast Morgan out. I'm tired of walking alone, of hiding, of pretending and forgetting myself in the sea of time. I want a place of my own with you at my side. Not you as a little woman, but you as a great big man, and you are going to help me get it. Do you understand?"

Stenibelle was half listening, half asleep, her body still trying to reconcile what had just happened to it. Morgan tapped her on the face.

"Are you listening? I just gave you something, now you are going to do something for me. You are going to go aboard the *George Parr* and you are going to get the information we both need. I'd get it myself, but it's haunted. There is Shadow tech all over that ship, it's contaminated with it, and I can't go there. So, you need to get it for me."

Morgan let her go and stood her up. Stenibelle was weak and wobbly, leaning against her. "Come on, get hold of yourself. I'm going to say something right now, and you better listen. You need the *Merthig*, There, I said it, and I can't believe it because I hate the *Merthig*. Everywhere I go, there's the *Merthig* in my way. Here, in Universe 3 as A-Ram and Alesta call it, in order to succeed, you need the *Merthig*. There, I said it again."

Stenibelle mumbled something.

"What's that? Speak up."

"I don't know what a *Merthig* is," Stenibelle said, her words slurred.

Morgan lost her patience. "Did you not listen to A-Ram and Alesta? The *Merthig!* The one who's at your side most of the bloody time. You draw power from the *Merthig*, and visa-versa. The *Merthig* can do things she couldn't ordinarily do because of you. It's all so cute and nice. Of all creatures, I hate the *Merthig* most. I'm jealous I guess—I want what the *Merthig* has. There, I said that too. I want to be the *Merthig* but I don't get to."

"But, what is it?"

"Not an *it*, it's a *who*. Gwendolyn, ok! It's Gwendolyn from Prentiss or Zenon or whatever, she's the *Merthig*!" Morgan stewed and seemed to be on the verge of a fit of temper. Her beauty faltered a bit. A hint of ugliness came through.

Stenibelle stammered, trying to awaken from her pleasured state. "But, what do you mean? To become friends with Lt. Gwendolyn? To become allies, compatriots?"

Morgan lost her temper. She shook Stenibelle. Her hands: the color had faded from her skin to a graveyard white. There were green, pitted claws, ridged and broken. "No, no, no, no, no! How wet are you? I don't mean become bosom buddies with Gwendolyn. I don't mean sharing a day at the park, trying on each-other's clothes, sitting by a friendly campfire roasting sweets as you giggle like little girls, you ignorant slag! I mean to *love* her, to *kiss* her, to stick your tongue down her mouth until you get to her tonsils, to get naked and roll in the hay while you strap on something provocative and illegal and go to it! That's what I'm talking about . . ."

"To become her lover? But, she's a woman. I'm not a man here, I'm a woman too."

"So?" Morgan screamed. She got up in Stenibelle's face, her eyes smoldering. "You're such a bore! '*Oh, she's a woman, it wouldn't be proper* . . .' Get past it! I could give you tips on maximizing a female-to-female encounter if you need some. I could teach you where to touch a woman to give her the maximum pleasure—I just showed you, didn't I? You need the *Merthig*. The *Merthig* gives you power. You need Gwendolyn and you need her in your bed."

Power?

The bloody kiss in the alley. The power she felt . . .

"I . . . hate her."

Morgan spat and was fed up. "I suggest you spit and shake on it, or settle up whatever issues you have. You know, I'm going to do you a big favor right now."

"What?"

"This . . ."

Stenibelle felt a wave of pure terror slam into her. It was enough to stop her heart. She fell to her knees, unable to function, unable to think. She looked up into Morgan's face.

The beautiful Morgan was gone. In her place was a twisted, ancient wretch, bone white and dusty, breasts sunk and knees bent, green claws ready to rip her apart, the face of an evil, toothy crone with the leering eyes of a wild animal. Her hair was a nest of green tangles. Stenibelle wanted to scream for Alesta but nothing came out but a terrified whimper.

"Like what you see? Like the immortal, ugly me?? Do you?" She raised her claws in a threatening manner. Fear hit Stenibelle in the face. She lost control of her bodily functions.

"Aw, you just peed yourself, how sweet." Morgan said in a callow voice. "You feel that? That's pure fear you're experiencing. Cool isn't it? Just a little parlor trick I can do."

Through gritted teeth, Stenibelle managed to talk. "W-what a-are you??"

"Me?" Morgan's eyes flashed. "I'm a monster, Bel, and I'm not kidding. I'm as bad as it gets. I'm no *Merthig*. I'm the *Tempus Findal*, the lonely one, the cursed one, the bookmarked page in some sage's book. I'm one who just ruins everything and takes the starch out of Kaidars like you. Right? Alesta said I'm 'somewhat' dangerous. Ha! If only! I'm completely, totally and utterly dangerous. I've been making men and women high and low quake with fear and pee their pants for ages. I can stop people's hearts if I want to. If you can stand against this, you can stand against anything. Now, I want you to stand up."

Stenibelle was soiled, locked in place, throat tightened, every bit of her bound up in fear, every beat of her heart surely her last.

"I said stand up!" Morgan roared. "Or I'll suck you out of existence right now and husk up and do all of this again in a century or two! You have five seconds. Stand up and live, or sit there and belly up to oblivion."

One, two . . .

Not possible. Not possible!!

three . . .

Stenibelle heard her sister's voice from somewhere deep down.

Get up, Bel!

Happy thoughts of the sand pit behind the manor, of her childhood, of going shoeless, dressing down in old linens and wrestling with Lyra in the pit. Mother would never approve, ladies did not wrestle. Their older sisters used the pit to make sand castles and fanciful palaces they hoped to one day live in with their husbands. But as soon as mother's back was turned, Lyra and Bel wrestled in the pit. They were going to be the boys their beloved father never had.

four . . .

Locking up with Lyra while Virginia watched, too shy to get in and wrestle with them. Headlocks and twisted ankles, bear hugging, grunting and straining, hair pulling, the occasional punch to the belly, the sand in their clothes and their faces, their mutually developing breasts proving to be more of a hindrance with each passing year. Lyra throwing her down. *"Get up, Bel,"* she would say.

And, always, she would get up, brush away the sand, and try again.

Stenibelle managed to move, managed to take command of her own fear-ridden body and make it move, force it to react. *"Let's go,"* she would say to Lyra. *"I'm ready for more."*

Slowly, she wobbled up and stood.

The beautiful Morgan was back, no more claws and bleached skin. She regarded her and smiled. She seemed impressed. The wall of fear abated and Stenibelle could breathe again. "Very good. If you can stand up to fear itself, then you've nothing to fear indeed."

She put her boots back on and headed to the door. "Remember what you felt just now and how you stood up to it. Seems like such a little thing, to stand up in the face of fear, you'd be amazed how many great men and women before you could not. No fear you will ever feel again will be like what I just did to you. Now, go and do your magic, and do not fail. If you do, the next time we meet, I might not be so nice to you. That's not a threat, it's just a truth."

And she exited and closed the door behind her.

✳   ✳   ✳   ✳   ✳

Blink . . . *Blink* . . . *Blink* . . .

The terminal flashed as Stenibelle sat down at the sparse desk in her room. Nervous, she swallowed hard and felt her mouth go dry. She had a crawling feeling she knew who was waiting for her on the other end.

After lunch, the Com Officer had informed her that she had a pending message. She wasn't expecting any messages, therefore, it could only be one person:

Hannah-Ben Shurlamp, either she or her associate Ottoman John, it had to be, and she wasn't ready to speak to either of them.

She cancelled the message and turned off her terminal. She would reach out to the Professor later when she was more composed and had prepared something to say, had some argument in her defense as to why she missed the *George Parr* on Planet Fall.

But, like a relentless demon forming in the corner, the terminal turned itself back on and, of its own accord "coned" into life.

Hannah-Ben Shurlamp was not to be denied and not even a turned off terminal on a Fleet ship millions of stellar miles away could stop her.

The cone formed. The grand finery that emerged was unmistakable, as was the powdered, bewigged woman in a snowy gown with raven tendrils and blaring brown eyes sitting behind the desk.

There she was, beautiful and regal, but just as scary as Morgan's ugly face. They stared at each other for a few moments.

Stenibelle spoke up. "Professor, well met. I had hoped to contact you later regarding . . . ."

Hannah-Ben Shurlamp coiled behind her desk. "Silence," she said, her voice tamed and cultured, but penned-in and raging just below the surface. "Lady Stenibelle. I do not appreciate my Coms going unanswered."

Stenibelle remained calm. She answered in a rational, composed manner. "You cut me off and left me stranded on Planet Fall. You know I had no money and no means of supporting myself."

"Then perhaps you should have been on that bloody ship as we agreed upon. I am not financing your ineptitude, not for one moment. I should have known you would prove to be a second-time failure. I had hoped there might be prospects for you, but look, see how you've blundered out of the gates, spending your idle time robbing and possibly whoring the dock-folk, yes I have the reports right here. Quite un-lady like, isn't it? Yes, cutting you off on barbaric Planet Fall was a reminder of who you are working for and how untenable your position is. Perhaps I should have had you arrested."

Elaborate holo-screens orbited her wigged head in an orderly fashion, and she glyphed them around with flicks from her wand. "And . . . no one fails me, do you understand? So, how shall I do it . . . what will the final hammer blow that seals the fate of the downtrodden House of Belmont-South Tyrol be? I'll leave it up to you. Which of your twenty-nine sisters shall I ruin first, or shall I start with your father and work backwards?"

Stenibelle was filled with panic. She spoke up. "You nearly killed me with those bolabungs. I was flat on my back fighting for my sanity. That's why I missed the *George Parr*. My health was compromised."

Professor Shurlamp pointed at Stenibelle with her glyph and it was like a poke in the chest. "You are a Tyrolese sorceress. You should be fully versed in the proper use of potent bolabungs. I hardly think I *need* or *should* be required to give you a primer on the matter; take it up with your schoolmasters if you require additional training. They were rare gifts intended to assist you, not for you to misuse and develop a terminal dependency. And now look . . . I think I shall first freeze the remaining assets of your House. Oh, tsk, look how pitifully low they are . . ."

"Wait!" Stenibelle roared. "I thought you wanted the location of Cammara?"

"Yes, and apparently I'll have it over your dead body."

Light from an open door spilled into Shurlamp's darkened study. The shadow of a portly man wearing a night shirt cast a dark smear on the wall. "For Creation's sake, Hannah, where are my goddamned spectacles? You know I cannot enjoy the posts without them?" came a nasally, rather whinny voice.

Hannah-Ben Shurlamp turned from her business. "They're on your nightstand, darling, as always."

"I looked there!"

"Just a moment, darling." Hannah-Ben turned back to Stenibelle. "Stand by a moment, please, I'll be back directly. Then I'll proceed to destroy your House."

She stood and gracefully exited the cone's field of view, her shadow joining the first one and elongating into a skeletal, demonic form. Stenibelle sat there trying to puzzle put a solution to this mess.

It was the *Seeker* all over again. Crushing indecision.

What to do? What can I do?

She racked her brains.

Soon the skeletal shadow reappeared, slithered down the wall and

Hannah-Ben Shurlamp returned and seated herself. "Now then, where were we? Ah yes . . . the end of your House."

"Professor, you cannot do this, please."

The Professor's brown eyes flashed up and locked onto Stenibelle's. "There is a hard price for failure, my dear." She picked her glyph back up. "Take this catastrophic event that is about to happen and learn from it."

Something unexpected happened at that moment. Instead of becoming paralyzed with fear and struck with selective mutism as she had in the past, Stenibelle found herself becoming annoyed, becoming angry. This time, she would not be bullied. She thought fast, all sorts of comebacks and responses formed in her thoughts.

"Wait! You wanted the data for Cammara, and I am in a position to get it for you. Isn't that what you want? Don't you have lectures to give and awards to receive?"

The Professor paused and tapped her fingers. "Are you saying you have it? Are you lying to me?"

"That's not what I'm saying. I'm saying I will have it shortly."

"And how so? The *George Parr* is at sea near Corvus. You are currently on a Fleet scouting ship making half-sail for Kana. What is your plan for boarding a Fleet ship at sea? The prime opportunity for your boarding was at Planet Fall, and that has passed."

"I have my methods. I shall be comfortably aboard their ship by the morrow and will have the information by nightfall."

The Professor regarded her with a critical eye. "Are you certain? I honestly don't see how you are going to accomplish this feat."

"I swear it. Prepare to be astounded."

The Professor sat back and tapped her glyph on the desktop. "Hmmm, I make you this counter-offer. I shall freeze the assets of one of your sisters, you may choose which. If you Com me from the *George Parr* by the morrow, then I shall reinvigorate her assets, no harm done and we shall proceed." She leaned forward. "So, which one is it to be?"

"Professor, this is not necessary."

"Yes it is. Pick one now or I shall stay up all night butcher-carving your House into an unrecognizable carcass floating down the river of Despair."

Stenibelle sighed. There appeared to be no mollifying the Professor, she wanted her writhing piece of collateral and there was no getting around it. The legion of her sisters rolled through her head, all regal, some like goddesses to her. She would not endanger Lyra and Virginia, they were precious to her and out-of-bounds. Beryla, Andromeda, Munni, Solona and Nylar, all social hierophants, wouldn't last two minutes without their husband's money and their lofty seats in League Society. Nathalie had spent years building her winery in Zenon, it was her dream. Constance was only recently cleared from the charge of witchcraft by the Sisters. Io and Miranda were only newly married.

The list went on and on

Who, who to ruin that would sting the least??

She had a thought. "My sister, Calami." She knew her older sister Calami lived a Spartan life in Remnath growing botanicals with her grimtooth husband. Her mother once complained: "*Calami, your Pewterlock-haired daughter, walked barefoot down the streets of St. Paris in a filthy dress, her hands caked in manure, and cared not who saw her.*"

Calami the Rebel. Calami the "I-Don't-Care" and bane of her mother. Of all her sisters, Calami could survive penniless the best. Calami was strong.

Hannah-Ben Shurlamp moved her glyph. "Done, and please choose one more sister, as Calami of Poole doesn't have any money to begin with. Freezing her paltry accounts really adds up to nothing."

Damn her! Stenibelle thought fast. "You did not specify the level of wealth or affluence of the sister I was to select. You asked for one sister and I gave you one. I insist you keep to your original demand. I love Calami no less than any of the others."

The Professor smiled a little. "Very well, what difference a day? Know this, I shall expect to hear from you aboard the *George Parr* by the morrow. Do you still have the Uni-Mind I gave you or did you lose that as well while you were robbing and whoring?"

Stenibelle showed the Professor her empty hand. She made a fist, and when she opened it again, the Uni-Mind was sitting in her palm. "Yes, I have it here."

Her use of Tyrol sorcery making the Uni-Mind appear from nowhere had no visible effect on the Professor. If she was impressed, she gave no indication. "Until tomorrow then, and if you fail, the rest of your sisters shall suffer a similar fate . . . and that is just the beginning. Do you understand?"

"Yes, I under—"

Hannah-Ben Shurlamp Commed off.

7—ALL ALONE

"Come in," Lt. Gwendolyn said.

The door meekly opened. Stenibelle entered Lt. Gwendolyn's tiny quarters, hat in hand. The walls were bare white paint on metal, riveted and ducted, sporting no personal effects whatsoever. The small bed in the back of the quarters was tightly made to military standards. The closet was filled with nothing but Fleet uniforms each identical to the next. Gwendolyn was sitting at her table, a deck of painted cards sitting scattered in front of her. The cheerful cards were the lone bit of color in the room.

"Captain, I was hoping for a moment of your time," Stenibelle said.

Gwendolyn extended a vacant hand. "Come."

Stenibelle wanted to sit down, but there wasn't another chair. She stood. "I wanted to thank you for allowing us this passage."

Gwendolyn responded in a dry voice. "Your fare was paid. You've kept to yourselves, you've not inconvenienced us or impeded the operations of this ship. You've no need to thank me."

Stenibelle had been avoiding this encounter all day.

"Bel, it would make me very happy if you would visit with Lt. Gwendolyn and offer your apologies for what was done on Planet Fall," Alesta had said. Stenibelle had come to love Alesta, and A-Ram, to depend on them both for strength and direction. Alesta had asked, and she could not refuse.

And, deep down, she knew Alesta was right—she owed Lt. Gwendolyn a sincere, unsolicited apology. It had taken her several dreadful hours pacing about in her room to generate the courage to stand before her.

"I wish to apologize for attacking you on Planet Fall. I want to say I'm sorry."

"We fought fair and square. I underestimated you and you beat me. I consider the matter closed." Gwendolyn locked eyes with her. It was brutal. "If you'd like to fight again, I assure you I will be more ready."

Stenibelle raised her hands. "Please, I don't want to fight you again."

With her hands in the air, she waved them back and forth in a quick manner. Gwendolyn's watch appeared in her hand from nowhere. "I want to give this back to you."

She held out the broken watch. Gwendolyn reached out and took it. "I had thought this lost," she remarked.

"I'm sorry I damaged it. May I compensate you for it so that you may buy a new one?"

Gwendolyn closed her eyes. "My watch cannot be replaced." She placed the watch on the table top. It sat there motionless like a corpse.

The two lingered there in silence.

The deed was done. Stenibelle had come to give the watch back and apologize, and Lt. Gwendolyn had listened. She had imagined offering a hastily-worded apology and then leaving as quickly as possible to the safety of her room.

Now that it was done, Stenibelle found herself not so eager to leave.

The kiss. The power.

In another universe, they loved each other.

The Merthig will give you power. Gwendolyn is the Merthig.

Put your tongue in her mouth . . . Morgan had said.

"May I see it for another moment, please?" Stenibelle asked.

Gwendolyn looked at her. "Why?"

"Just for a moment, please."

Gwendolyn slowly slid the watch across the tabletop. The crystal face was cracked, the mechanism damaged.

"May I ask where this watch came from? It obviously means a great deal to you."

"It was a gift."

"You gave it to her," came Alesta's words.

Stenibelle shook her hands and produced a fine set of lock picks and other precision tools and laid them out on the table. Gwendolyn watched her conjure these items up from nowhere without surprise or interest. She seemed lost, or in another place.

"I think I can fix this," she said. Stenibelle turned the watch over and skillfully removed the back plate exposing the damaged workings within. That seemed to catch Gwendolyn's interest.

"Are you a watchmaker?" Gwendolyn asked, studying her as she worked.

"No," she said, "but I was taught to be skilled with my hands." She selected a few tools from her kit and began working.

"This seems beyond repair to me."

"Who gave this to you?" Stenibelle asked again, already knowing the answer. "Was it someone dear to you?"

Gwendolyn sat quiet and didn't say anything.

"Captain?"

"If you must know, I was given my watch by a person from my dreams. I'm certain that sounds rather silly, doesn't it? A proper daughter of Prentiss and Zenon does not dwell on dreams, but, one night, there he was. I saw him in my dreams standing by my bed, and then the next morning there was my watch, sitting on the nightstand." Gwen paused, puzzled. "I can't rightly recall having ever told anyone that before. My parents and my sisters often question me on the matter, wondering who the mystery man is, but I've always remained mum. Why did I just tell you, I wonder?"

Stenibelle turned her eyes up from her work for a moment. "Perhaps we are closer than you might think. I thank you for sharing that with me."

I gave it to you, Gwen, and then I took it away. Gwendolyn had a large, square face. Stenibelle mused: *I probably couldn't get my tongue half-way to your tonsils, even if I tried.*

She sighed. "Have you ever had a dream so wonderful, Lady Belmont, that it makes every moment afterwards unbearable? Have you?"

"I think I have, yes," Stenibelle agreed.

"I've looked for this man. He must exist, my watch exists. I've spent hours in Fleetcom searching for him, describing his features to the database. Nothing is ever found. I cannot locate him, he's just a ghost."

"And, you've fallen in love with this man from your dreams?"

Gwendolyn's hand went to her breast for a moment, and then fell. A bit of naked emotion came out across her face and then retreated back within. She nodded. "I will love no other." She looked hard at Stenibelle. "Your eyes are like his. Same shade, same patterns, same bits of light and dark."

Stenibelle blinked. "You can see that much detail all the way across the table?"

"I have Sight like no other. I can see like a Vith. I can see your beating heart in your chest and the VUNKULA you have hidden under your coat." Gwendolyn seemed puzzled. "Why am I telling you these things, my deepest secrets? Who are you? We fought not days ago and you broke my watch. I should hate you, but I don't. I've not had issues hating people in the past, and for lesser offences. Maybe it's because your eyes are like his."

Gwendolyn has the Sight? Only the Vith have the Sight, like Captain Davage. A-Ram told her: *As a Merthig, Gwendolyn will be able to do things she wouldn't ordinarily be able to do. She derives that ability from her connection to you. It's a symbiotic relationship, you give each other power.*

"Perhaps that man you seek is closer than you think." Stenibelle adjusted the workings and repaired several springs. She put everything back into place with minute skill. She gave it a shake and the watch began ticking again, moving with a precise beat. "See, anything can be fixed, Captain. It just takes a little effort." She picked the watch up and held it out.

Gwendolyn extended her hand to take it. Their hands touched.

"Allow me to offer a parting gesture for luck," Stenibelle said as she held Gwendolyn's hand. "Just a simple offering we have in Tyrol expressing my hope that your watch continues to beat." She swept her fingertips across the watch face and Gwendolyn's palm and then gave two light raps with her knuckles. "We call it the 'Wishluck' gesture. Just a small touch that means a great deal to us."

Gwendolyn stared at her hand. She took her watch and put it back on her wrist. She seemed to be a thousand miles away, lost once again in her own head, searching for a phantom. "I'm sorry, I should have offered you my chair. Where are my manners?"

"It's all right."

Stenibelle put her tools away and took her hat. "I still owe you a new crystal, and I assure you I will make good on it." She slowly turned and headed to the door.

She stopped. There was much to be said. She carried many of the secrets Gwendolyn had longed for. She was the answered prayer, the end of the journey. She was the phantom man, the watchman of Gwendolyn's dreams.

Stenibelle hadn't wanted to come, now she didn't wish to leave. She felt a connection, a tiny but unbreakable cord connecting her soul to Gwendolyn's, a cord that spanned the universes. All the hate she had felt for seven months was gone, replaced by something else, something quiet but persistent and unavoidable. Alesta and Morgan were right.

You and the Merthig . . .

"I'm to be leaving soon when we make berth. I'll not be back," Stenibelle said. No reaction from Gwendolyn.

"I want to give you something first. It's not much, but still, it taught me an important lesson and perhaps it will do the same for you . . ."

"You've already given me my watch."

"I have more to give." She waved her hand and set a small photo on the table. She slid it toward her.

"What's this?" Gwendolyn asked turning her attention away from her watch.

"It's a photo I was given, and now I want to give it to you in turn."

Gwendolyn took it and held it in front of her face. She studied it. "I recognize Lord A-Ram, and Lady Alesta, and there I am. I don't recall ever being photographed with either of them." Her eyes locked onto the tall handsome image of Stenibelle as a man. They widened. "Who is this man? Who is he? He's dressed like you." Gwen's eyes peeked over the top of the picture and fell on Stenibelle. "I notice a resemblance, is this man your brother, perhaps?"

"Do you recognize him?"

"I do. I know his face." She appeared a bit desperate. "Please tell me you know who he is."

"Is that the man from your dreams?"

"Yes, yes he is. Do you know him? Do you know where he may be found?"

Stenibelle answered. "I do know him. That man is not my brother, Lady Gwendolyn. I have no brothers. The man you see in the photo is me in a different reality, so I'm told."

Gwendolyn was puzzled. "Another reality? I don't believe in such things. There is no reality besides this one."

"That's what I once thought as well, but I have been taught different. There are many places, many realities. I am just now coming to terms with such a prospect. Look at the photo. It's true. That is you, and the man standing there beside you is me. And look at us . . . In another place look how we love each other. Can you not see it in the photo? See that same watch on your wrist? I gave it to you. I came to you in your dreams, though I was a man. These are truths I have come to know."

Gwendolyn didn't reply. She stared at the picture with a hard, empirical expression. As her eyes moved up and down her expression changed a bit: softer, more unsure and quizzical, trying to make sense of it. She was no longer in her hidden place. She was now right in front of her listening with full attention.

"The watch, I'm told, is a gift I gave to you to commemorate the occasion of our engagement. I bought it in a fine jeweler's mark on Hoban. I wanted to give you a practical gift, something you could use every day. I . . ."

Gwendolyn flushed a little and Stenibelle stopped. "I see you," she said. "I'm listening. I know lies from truth. Are you lying to me?"

"No."

"Then tell me more."

Stenibelle looked around at the bare walls and cold metal of her quarters and felt closed-in by it all. "I wish I had more to tell. In many places I am a man. Here, I am a woman."

She reached out across the table and gently took Gwendolyn by the cheek, allowing her fingers to explore the soft passes of her skin.

She felt her fingers react to the touch. A slight sting and a trail of stirred memories.

The power the Merthig gives you . . .

"I'm sorry, Gwen. I'm sorry that, here, I'm not the man you love, the man who gave you that watch. I'm sorry I'm not that person for you. I'm sorry you're all alone."

"You need the Merthig, and the Merthig needs you . . ." Morgan had said with considerable bile and envy.

Her watch ticked. Gwendolyn sat down and looked at the picture, fading back into that private world she appeared to inhabit most of the time. Stenibelle turned and took her leave, opening the door and passing through it, the latch fastening with a cold metallic clunk.

The touch. The feeling it gave.

As she closed the door, she lingered a moment. She heard the dim ghost of bitter weeping drifting out from within.

You need the Merthig and the Merthig needs you.

A woman??

Get past it!

She leaned against the door and put her hands to her heart. It was the most sorrowful sound Stenibelle had ever heard.

∗　∗　∗　∗　∗

A day later the *Demophalon John* landed them via Ripcar in the center of nowhere somewhere in the midlands of Kana and then took its leave. To the south were a line of soft purple mountains and patchy stands of fir trees. The terrain was very unfamiliar to Stenibelle, used to the windswept coasts and flat interior swamplands of Tyrol. "Where in the name of Creation are we?"

Morgan-Jeterix stood nearby. "Vithland, Bel. Never been here before?"

"I haven't—and please don't tell me that I knew this place in another reality, because it's really irrelevant."

Morgan rolled her eyes and thought about it. "I have no idea, actually."

"Well, that's a relief."

Morgan pointed to the south-west. "My home in Hala was that way, about a thousand miles. There's green good land in that direction across the mountains."

"Was?" Stenibelle asked.

"Yeah, that was about fifteen or sixteen thousand years ago, I can't quite remember. It's pretty much just a cursed field now where nobody goes. It's too creepy for them."

Alesta and A-Ram got their bearings. "Excellent. This is a good spot, yes. Here, I can call the Road. Rammy, can you help me?" she asked as she unbuttoned her boots. A-Ram went to her and she leaned against him.

Alesta pulled her boots off and gave them to A-Ram. "Now, I shall call The Road and transport you, Bel, to the *George Parr*. Give me a moment." She seated herself and raised her arms, the green sleeves of her robe falling down to her elbows. Stenibelle watched with interest.

A-Ram approached her. "It will take Alesta a few minutes to summon the Road. While we're waiting let me go over everything with you again, alright? While you were recovering from your bout with the bolabungs, we managed to get permission to board the *George Parr* and go inside. Alesta has to have seen with her own eyes the location she wishes to travel to, and, in this case, all we got to see was Deck 4. So, that's where you're going to end up: Deck 4 near the aft of the ship. You're going to want to be Faded into the Shadows in case anybody happens to be passing so they won't see you."

"Alright. No problem."

"Secondly, be very careful when going through locked doorways. I know you can pick the locks with ease, but doing so will trigger an alarm at the Com station on the bridge and they'll become alerted to your presence. Don't pick the locks if you don't absolutely have to."

"I remember that, thank you, A-Ram."

"Good. Now, here's the last thing. We will not be able to retrieve you off the ship. There's too much energy and power generated by the vessel. Alesta can deposit you there, but she cannot summon the Road to the ship. The power won't allow the Road to form like it needs to. It would be nice if we could."

Stenibelle laughed. "It would save us all a lot of trouble, wouldn't it? You needn't worry." She reached into her HRN and pulled out a handful of three Brown Holystones. She initially had several dozen, but after her robbing and kidnapping exploits on Planet Fall, she was down to three. "Remember these? These will summon a Black Maiden who, in turn, will return any coated in its scent to my little work area on Planet Fall. That is how I shall exit the *George Parr* once I have the location of Cammara."

"Ok, don't lose those, whatever you do. We will be watching from afar and will do what we can to help you."

Stenibelle affectionately tapped him on the cheek. "Thanks. It'll make me feel secure knowing you're watching over me."

From the north, a fog lifted and rolled in. Stenibelle felt a chill on the wind.

"The Road comes. It's almost time." A-Ram said. "Are you sure you have everything?"

Stenibelle checked her HRN: its hidden pockets were full of Holystones and MARZABLE and other kit. Her VUNKULA was coiled and her Grenville 40 sat snug in her sash. Professor Shurlamp's Uni-Mind was safe in its pocket. "Yes, I'm ready."

She glanced at Morgan. She was bursting with new confidence, and some of it she attributed to Morgan's "fear-soak".

"I'm sorry I'm such a square."

Morgan chuckled. "S'all right. I'm traveling myself here soon. You'll not see me again, but you will."

Stenibelle absorbed that for a moment, had no idea what she was talking about and disregarded it. "Well then excellent. I wish you luck with me, wherever I am. I think that cold thing you did will be a big hit."

"Would you like another jolt, for old time's sake?" Morgan smiled wickedly.

"No, thank you."

A-Ram was cross. "What 'jolt', Morgan?"

"Nothing, nothing . . . Just helping out."

Dubious, A-Ram gave Stenibelle a hug and she hugged him back. "It's time. Be safe, Bel."

"I will, A-Ram. Promise." Before she let him go, she took his hand and did her usual Tyrol Wish-Luck gesture, just a gentle swipe across his palm with her fingers and a few knocks with her knuckles. "Speedwell, my friend, and thank you for everything." She Faded into the Shadows and disappeared from sight.

The fog rose up and formed into a long tunnel. Morgan and A-Ram then stepped back as the fog closed in and thickened. Stenibelle was lost in the fog, had no idea which way was which. She saw Alesta look back and open her mouth to say something, and then she was gone.

Stenibelle was standing alone in a bare corridor. It was at least ten degrees warmer than where she'd just been standing. She was on the *George Parr*, Deck 4, somewhere near the aft end of the ship just as A-Ram said. Silent and at the blink of an eye she had travelled millions of stellar miles onto a moving ship at sea. She heard the distant throb of a well-running thermoplant and smelled the cool murkiness of processed, scrubbed oxygen.

Invisible, she was alone. The deck was a bit shorter in height than that of a *Triumph*-class vessel, indicating it was a smaller class of ship. The floor was carpeted in a standard Fleet weave of a somber reddish color, the plumbing was exposed in blanketed pipes and she didn't see any lock-in stations for the crew to use during battle. She was used to the lavish and, by comparison, posh environs of a *Triumph*-class ship where she once served as Paymaster. This seemed more workman-like and utilitarian, like a scouting ship, like Lt. Gwendolyn's ship.

Gwendolyn. She was now very far from Gwendolyn.

The corridor was clear. She checked her watch: 18 Bells. She had to get a Com out to Professor Shurlamp as soon as possible, that was her first task and she had to do it without alerting the Com Officer on the bridge. Like a hitch in her thoughts, like the confused onset of a stroke, the Professor's Ceril-Cone information bubbled up and barged in. Deck 4: a habitation deck. This is where the crew lived in their small billets. All around her were closed doors, one after the other like a small, unadorned inn. She didn't hear any talking coming from the billets or sounds of holo or Airenet. Nobody came in or out of the doors. The whole place had a vacant feel to it and she didn't like it much.

She tried one of the doors. It was locked. Not a surprise. Inside of every one of these billets was an unsecured Com terminal, just waiting for her to use. The safe return of her sister Calami's assets was just a picked lock away.

A-Ram's warning flashed through her head: *don't pick the locks.*

She had to get into one of these billets and she also had to stay undetected. She decided to wait a few minutes, somebody was sure to come by, this was a working Fleet vessel full of 157 crew and officers and here was the heart of where they lived. She would wait, when somebody passed by, she would invisibly follow them into their billet and give them a quick kiss from her VUNKULA. She moved it within the folds of her coat, dipping the clawed tip into a pocket full of sleeping powder. She was ready.

She waited. Time passed.

Nobody came by.

What is going on, she wondered. Where is everybody? The corridor was still, save the steady thrum of the thermoplant. Where was the knocking about, the hints of conversation, the opening or closing of a door, the regular cacophony of small comforting sounds people made? As she waited and became uneasy, she wondered if anybody was on this ship at all. She wondered if she was the only soul aboard. Having sailed on the *New Faith*, she often listened to the scary, spine-tingling stories the crew liked to tell of lost ships, cursed ships.

Ghost ships.

She remembered the one of the lost freighter, *Mysti Parker,* stumbling through the empty sea lanes of the League with no crew and no reasonable explanation as to what happened to them. Just gone, people gone. That story, those empty decks, the over-turned chairs, the abrupt lack of human habitation and all the souls lost at sea unburied and unanointed in death, truly terrified her.

Perhaps the *George Parr* was a ghost ship too. What had Morgan said? *Ship's haunted.*

She wondered if A-Ram and Alesta were watching. "This really stinks, guys." She waved up her three brown Holystones, her ticket off the ship. Feeling them in her hand comforted her.

She didn't want to stand there any further. Stenibelle decided to quit Deck 4 and proceed to the main mess. Once there, her plan was to select a crewman from those present. She would then follow the crewman back to their billet wherever that was, incapacitate them, then make her all-important Com to Professor Shurlamp. Then, she'd move on to the Captain and Rodrigo of Burgon, gather the data she needed and get off this accursed ship. She put her Holystones away and readied to move out.

The Ceril information, though ill-fitting and uneasy in her head, was amazing. Her knowledge of the ship was complete, as if she'd worked on it for ten years. Thankfully leaving the dreary quiet of Deck 4, she went up two decks and drifted toward the main mess hall, passing nobody along the way. The Ceril information was a bad guest in her head. It blanked her thoughts, it scrambled her memories and poked her in the eye from behind. It also made her hallucinate. Seeing new things as she made her way triggered the Ceril, bumping in her head like a lunatic, rewriting the open slate of her thoughts. She thought she saw someone every so often, standing in the distance, a tall figure in a dark blue Fleet uniform that faded as fast as she'd seen it. As she moved, she became aware of a strange smell floating about, an earthy, dirty smell. It wasn't a sterile, approved smell one would expect to encounter on a starship. Starships smelled exactly how the Admiralty wanted them to smell. This was a harsh smell, an ugly one, like rotten meat.

It smelled like something was dead. Maybe the smell was a Ceril-inspired hallucination too, but she didn't think so. She quickened her pace.

The mess was empty when she arrived. She fully expected the usual bustle of crew both coming off their shifts and preparing to begin. Life aboard a starship could be boring and dreary sometimes, and the mess hall was usually the heart of the ship where the crew could engage in a bit of merriment and frivolity as they took their meals. The mess was never empty.

Here though, nothing. The tables and chairs were unoccupied. The galley was shut down, all the machinery was covered with a series of tarps lashed together. A basket of unappetizing wrapped sandwiches, a machine vending bagged kelsos and another serving various cans of hot and cold beverages were all that was there. The cans on display in the vending machine reminded her of a line-up of little tombstones.

Stenibelle was at a loss. Seeing this place empty when it should have been seething with life was quite soul-shattering for her. She didn't understand, and she had to make that Com to the Professor. Nothing made sense. She felt the harsh stirrings of hysteria rattling around within her.

Footsteps outside. The sound startled her. She drew her Grenville 40 and stepped back against the wall.

What would come through the door, a human, a monster or a ghost?

To her relief a male crewmen entered. At last! She felt she wanted to kiss him.

You're here! You exist!

But, as she took in the sight of him, her previous state of unease returned. This man didn't look like a Fleet crewman. His uniform was unkempt, his face and hair mussed. He was like a scabrous ghoul sloppily wearing a uniform. He selected a sandwich from the basket and pulled a can of water from the machine. Without saying a word he turned and headed back out the door passing right by her not seeing a thing, her Fade into the Shadows at least was properly working and he had no supernatural powers to detect her. Stenibelle followed him.

He moved down the corridor, slouching, rubbing his belly, going down three decks. More Ceril puttered around giving her the grand tour of the ship whether she wanted it or not.

Another hallucination somebody was standing there in a side corridor. It was Gwendolyn, she was certain of it. She stood there holding her hands to her eyes, cupping her fingers like a pair of binoculars, looking through them.

I see you . . .

And she was gone.

He entered a large room. More confusion, more Ceril-Cone information claiming her headspace, slapping down any other less important thoughts. It told her she was in Hold 1. The man sat down at a desk and unwrapped his sandwich. Stenibelle got a good look at the man as he ate. He wasn't registering in her Ceril-Cone. There couldn't be any way Hannah-Ben Shurlamp would miss a crewman. He must be new. Given his gruff appearance, the Captain must be loose in the extreme with his standards.

Something was very wrong on this ship, and she wanted to know what it was. Invisible and undetected, she continued on into the hold to have a quick look around.

The hold was full of dozens of containers, all long and cylindrical, stacked up high. That smell, that horrible dead smell, came from the containers, it was enough to sicken her.

These containers are just big enough to be a coffin.

They had an ominous feel to them, as if something frightening was hidden inside. Though she didn't want to, she decided she needed to look inside and see what she was dealing with. She didn't want to be surprised with anything later on.

Morgan-Jeterix, face of a crone and reaching with pitted claws might come out.

She waded into the rows, selecting one at a convenient height. The lid was locked. The container didn't appear to be connected to anything that would give her position away if she opened it. She sashed her Grenville 40. A quick shake of the hand had her lock picks out. She worked the lock. After several seconds she had the lock picked and carefully swung the lid open. A terrible, earthy stench billowed out making her gag.

It's Morgan!

A female body was housed snuggly within the container. She was wearing the uniform of a Fleet crewman. Her curly brown hair, damp with sweat, was wrapped around her face. Her shoulders were slightly too wide for the container and were stuffed in at an uncomfortable oblong angle. Stenibelle reached in, brushed her hair aside and saw her face. Ceril knowledge bubbled in: it was Crewman Lessa, Lady of Walpole, Assistant Regular in the ship's Audio/Visual Department.

Was she dead? Was she the victim of some sort of space-borne malady? The woman was alive, but she was burning up, Stenibelle could feel the heat radiating off her. If she was sick, why wasn't she being treated? There weren't any medicality in there with her, no bagged fluids, no scanners or bio-devices, no encrypted diagnosis and assessments on a chip. She was simply stuffed into a box (and not a medical stasis unit, just a standard cargo container) and shut in like a bolt of cloth. Why wasn't she taken off the ship and Hospitalered? That's how the Fleet handled the sick, especially within the core of the League where treatment was easily reachable. The sick were not stored in the hold in a box.

She looked around: dozens of containers all around her just like this one. Did each of those also contain a body??

"What's going on out there?" came a voice. "Who's there? I heard you!" The man overseeing the hold set his sandwich down and came to investigate. With a drawn Hertamer Heat gun, he came wandering into the rows. She was still faded into the Shadows, so he didn't see her, but he saw the open container and he also saw Stenibelle's lockpick set. He picked it up, puzzled.

"What the frag is this?"

FHATOM!

Stenibelle struck with her VUNKULA and got him in the neck, dosing him good with a revised, much less caustic sleep powder that Morgan had helped her create while on the *Demophalon John* with supplies bought by A-Ram and Alesta. Stenibelle would not forget the money she owed them.

She harbored the nightmare thought that this man was a ghoul and would resist her sleeping powder, that he would stand there and laugh, teeth bared, eyes crazed, and tear her apart. But, he fell forward and dropped to the floor seconds later, his weapon clattering from his limp fingers. He was just a man.

Time was running out. She formed a plan. According to Professor Shurlamp's Ceril knowledge, Lady Lessa's billet was only a deck away, on the accursed Deck 4. She could go in and use her unsecured Com terminal and possibly not be noticed by the Com Officer on the bridge. She would need Lady Lessa to open the palm lock on the door. She indulged in the quick and rather lurid scenario of chopping Lessa's hand off and taking it with her, but dismissed it. Had she still been Bunged-Up, that's what she would have done.

She dragged the limp body of Lady Lessa out of the container and allowed her to ooze face down to the floor. She had a moment of inspiration—she'd use the man's workstation to make the Com. She turned to the horrid unconscious crewman and planned to stuff him in the container, slamming the lid on the bugger. Gods but was he heavy. The VUNKULA snaked out of her coat and gripped the man by his collar. Bracing herself, the VUNKULA lifted and dumped him in, his arms and legs sticking out of the sides like a gangly marionette. She stuffed in his arms and legs, placed a pink Holystone in his palm to keep him out, and shut the lid.

So much for him. Stenibelle checked his workstation. The invasive Ceril information that slapped her in the face wasn't good news—no Com terminal, just a shipboard interlink. Plan B: get to Lessa's billet. She scooped Lessa up and carried her fire brigade style over her shoulders. She wondered what would happen should she encounter anybody along the way, the random passerby seeing a woman floating bent over on air. It might make for a memorable scene, but, as before, she encountered no one.

Back to haunted, lonely Deck 4, this time in the company of an unconscious, fevered crewman. As the Ceril tap-danced through her head, she saw Gwendolyn a few more times, always standing in the distance looking at her.

"I'll talk to you in a little bit, Gwen, I promise," she muttered.

Here was Lessa's billet, #47S. Her back was aching from the carry.

Stenibelle manhandled her limp body up with the VUNKULA and managed to get her hand to the palm lock. The door fell open, revealing a dark interior. She dragged the woman in and closed the door behind her. It occurred to her that opening the door with the palm lock would also trigger a readout on the Com station, not an alarm, just a passing bit of information that she hoped the Com officer wouldn't notice. Too late now, they were in. The room was freezing, the heat had been turned off. That was also a problem. Their combined body heat could rapidly raise the temperature of the room and signal the bridge yet again. She dragged the woman into the bathroom and rolled her into the shower. She hoped the cold tiles would help reduce her temperature. That done, she went back out into the room. On a nearby desk was the crewman's Fleet Com terminal—at last, from here she could reach Professor Shurlamp and get Calami her assets back.

She made her way to the crewman's Com Terminal and fired it up. She produced the Uni-Mind, got it out of its pouch and set it down on the desktop. After a moment, it sprouted stalk-like silvery legs and moved on its own toward the terminal. More legs came out and it interfaced with the terminal at withering speed, bypassing Fleet security and finding a secure line out of the ship. The codes it used triggered an amazing amount of relaying, jumping from point to point, arriving at a restaurant in Hoban, bouncing off of several freighters in space, continuing on, moving too rapidly for Stenibelle to follow. With luck, the transmission would not be noticed by the bridge.

Eventually the now familiar study and desk of Hannah-Ben Shurlamp, paneled and padded in splendid finery, appeared on the screen surrounded by the usual bewildering array of floating holographic screens. Given the abandoned state of the *George Parr*, given the haunted corridors, the unearthly stench, the hold full of bodies and the ghoul-like crewman, seeing the grounded, concrete Professor in her wallpapered study was a relief. It helped beat back the lonely hysteria with a dose of solid, tangible reality.

Professor Shurlamp sat there in her snowy white gown with her perfect, ladylike posture. Her eyes flicked across her screens. "Lady Stenibelle, right on time . . . and I see you are indeed aboard the *George Parr* as promised." She checked and double checked several of the floating holographic screens moving with army-like precision about her head, her brown eyes darting from one screen to another. "Yes, well done. I am quite impressed. I had my calendar cleared this evening so that I could destroy your House uninterrupted."

"Then release my sister's assets at once," she said.

The Professor shook her Glyph. "Done. See, that was easy, wasn't it? Now then, I want the coordinates to Cammara and any other materials you happen upon by this evening Kana standard. I will wait no longer."

Stenibelle bristled. She was tired of cowing and being dictated to. In her previous encounters with the Professor, she had been dominated, intimidated, humbled and at a general loss for words. Now, after Morgan's "fear-soak", she didn't feel intimidated at all. As Morgan had said, no fear could ever equal the fear she'd been subjected to on the *Demophalon John*, and she felt almost nothing. She went on the offensive, her tongue wagging quite before she could stop it.

"You, madam, will wait until I am good and ready to give you the information, understand? I am to see Rodrigo of Burgon soon. He has the information, and then I'll have it."

"I'll expect the information first thing in the morning then. And, I'd tread carefully, for Rodrigo of Burgon has a number of vile fungal infections best avoided if possible, should you choose to get the information out of him via sex."

Stenibelle was disgusted at the thought. She set herself and put the fear-soak to the test. "First, Professor, we've some bargaining to do, don't we?"

Hannah-Ben Shurlamp sat back. "Do we? Consider your House "

"I am always considering my House. I'm considering it even at this very moment. Consider your shame when someone else takes the credit for rediscovering Cammara. I can see it clearly, you sitting in a vast audience with your plate of tasteless catered food growing cold in front of you as you politely clap with the others in the crowd as the spotlight turns to the stage illuminating someone else. Imagine . . ."

The Professor put down her glyph and regarded Stenibelle for a moment. She appeared somewhat impressed that Stenibelle actually had the gall to stand up to her. "I see. Yes, that is quite the picture, isn't it? What do you want, then?"

"I was offered five million sesterces by a rival of yours."

"Five million? Is that all? What rival of mine would be so pinchy with their payouts, I wonder?" She picked her glyph back up. "Shall I place the money in your personal account or in the general Belmont House coffers?"

"No, no, you don't understand. I want thirty million. And, the general House coffers will do."

The Professor gave her a scalding look.

Stenibelle heard a small whimpering coming from the bathroom. Lady Lessa must be stirring. "How much is the secret worth to you, I wonder?" she said, keeping the pressure up.

Hannah-Ben Shurlamp smiled and adjusted her wig. She moved her glyph again. "Very well, thirty million sesterces have been deposited. I must say, you do learn fast, Lady Stenibelle. Very admirable. But, I wouldn't advise you to test me much further. If you're planning on creating some sort of bidding war between myself and an anonymous second party, I would entreat you to not get greedy. Greed has its time and place, and it is not now. Allow me to compliment you. You have proved yourself capable and resourceful, and I appreciate those things. If you get me the data, there shall be more money to come, much more, rest assured—more than you could possibly know what to do with. You'll find I am a kind benefactor with unlimited resources. Use the Uni-Mind. If Rodrigo of Burgon has the data encrypted on a device of some sort, then the Uni-Mind will dig it out. Now then, I don't mind paying the price for trustworthy people, and as long as you serve me, I shall, in turn, serve you. I can answer any question you have, I can supply you with anything you need, I can keep the wolves away from your House's throat and I can back you up with an army if need be. I am a person you want on your side. My side is the winning side. Conversely, I am a deadly enemy when crossed, you must understand that by now. Don't cross me and accept all that I have to offer and we shall both prosper. I shall be here around the clock awaiting your transmission."

She Commed off.

Stenibelle took a moment to be proud of herself. "Well, A-Ram and Alesta, if you're listening, looks like I've got a pair of balls after all. Thanks for showing them to me."

8—Crew in Limbo

Now that that was out of the way and Calami had her meager assets restored to her, it was time to make some headway regarding this mystery. Captain Duval's quarters would be located in the executive wing near the bridge, Deck 2.

Another sound came from the bathroom. Perhaps the crewman was waking up? She drew her Grenville 40 and went in. The crewman had managed to somehow turn on the water and crawl partially out of the shower and was slumped face-down on the tiles. Stenibelle turned off the water and knelt down to check her. She was sopping wet, her hair drenched. She turned her over. Her body was freezing from the cold water in the shower, but, behind the topical cold was the roaring heat of her body threatening to reassert itself. The crewman was still unconscious, yet she must have come to, at least for a moment, as her left hand was partially thrust into her pocket. Stenibelle carefully pulled her hand out.

A data crystal nestled in her limp fingers clattered to the floor.

Standing over the fallen crewman, Stenibelle was reminded of Gwendolyn lying bloody on the cold metal street of Planet Fall.

The sounds of Gwendolyn weeping behind the metal door passed through her thoughts, haunting them.

I'm so sorry, Gwen . . .

As she stood there she began having the first vague notions of feeling sorry for the poor crewman. She hadn't intended to interact with the crew at all, but here she was, sopping wet in front of her. And, for that matter, what was wrong with her? She was not asleep, and, had she been mildly drugged, the cold water should have rousted her out.

Damn!

She dragged the girl from the bathroom and wrangled her into bed. She stripped and dried her with a towel. She checked her closet: several changes of clothing hung from a rack, along with a few uniforms, boots and shoes neatly arranged in a pigeon-hole waiter, and a plump terrycloth robe. An elaborate float camera sat on the floor, turned off and forgotten. She fetched the robe to keep her from catching a chill.

Her mission aboard this ship was clear, but her mother had taught her to be curious and to puzzle out a pressing problem until it was solved. Something sinister was at work aboard this ship and she had to know what she was dealing with. Perhaps, had she still been wearing her Bolabungs, she wouldn't have cared, she was here for data, for Cammara and the well-being of her House, not the crew. But, the Bolabungs were gone and thankfully so, and Stenibelle's heart spoke.

Help this person if you can.

She went through the crewman's drawers and closet. She found her Fleet ID: Crewman Standard Lessa of Tharpoli, Lady of the Onaris House of Walpole and a junior assistant in the ship's AV department; the Professor's Ceril-Cone information was spot-on. She wondered about the creepy guy she'd imprisoned in the hold, there was no Ceril information on him at all.

Why?

Moving on, she checked her drawers for evidence of drugs, arcane tinctures or salves.

Nothing.

She went back into the bathroom to check her medicine chest and kicked the data crystal across the floor.

The crystal. It must mean something to her. She had it in her pocket and she had, if only for a moment, revived a bit and sought it out. Stenibelle got the Uni-mind. Tiny legs came out and seized the crystal, moving it around. A holographic cone came up and the data came through. It was a vast collection of photos and vids showing a smiling Lady Lessa with her friends. There she was, waving, apparently quite gregarious making ample use of her free time, some of her friends in the pictures were Fleet crewmen like she was. There were a long series of pictures of herself on Bazz, by the beaches, splashing in the warm water with her pant-legs rolled up, sampling the hot local fare, trying on lacy Bazz clothing in the marketplaces and making silly faces for the camera with her friends.

Ah, look here, frequent photos of herself and a handsome gentleman, himself also a Fleet crewman. There they were swimming together, shopping in the Bazz sunshine; him bogged down with packages, him hand feeding her something red and unbearably hot at a cafe. Here was a photo of Lady Lessa wearing a floppy hat while in the gentleman's embrace. They appeared to be sharing a kiss, though the brim of her hat covered their faces from the camera's eye.

So, here she seemed a perfectly vivacious young lady with a love of camaraderie and picture-taking enjoying the sights and ports of call her Fleet duty bought her to and also enjoying the company of a young man. So, what happened? How had she ended up in a container in the hold like a cargo full of spoiled meat? She checked the date stamp on the photos. They went back several years with numerous photos and vids being taken at steady, regular intervals. The most recent picture was taken several weeks prior, and then they stopped all together—nothing more. The last picture was interesting. Lessa had taken a photo of a procession of strange, robed, slightly stunted people filing out of the Ripcar bay. Looking at the photo, the robed people had an ominous presence, their skin, what little she could see of it, had an orange hue. That was the last image before the end-of-file marker.

The Uni-Mind released the crystal and Stenibelle returned it to her HRN.

Something terrible had happened since the last picture was taken, and, Stenibelle had to assume all the rest of the containers she saw in the hold also contained crewmen in a similar state.

Stenibelle checked Crewman Lessa again. Her temperature appeared to be quite high. Stenibelle guessed she had a fever of 102 to 104. She checked her for signs of drugging or poisoning: no drooling (which sometimes happened), no odd smells or aromas. Her breathing was nice and steady. Her heartbeat, however, was troubling. Her heart was racing. She shook her hand and produced a pinkie, placing it into her palm. The effects of the pinkie should calm her system and slow her heart rate a little. Without the pinkie her heart might have run away to over two hundred beats per minute. An accelerated heartbeat was a clear symptom of being under the influence of a spell.

Looking further, Lessa had on no arcane jewelry or trinkets that might have locked her into a spell, no bolabungs. Using her thumbs she gently lifted one of her eyelids. Her pupils were unresponsive to light. She was, without question, under the influence of something external.

Hmmm, look here. She bore an odd black tattoo on her left shoulder which appeared to be of arcane origins. It was composed of twisting lines, dots and intersecting points. Her training told her that tattoos could be used to impart a spell upon a person; the ink used could have certain effects, the ceremonies enacted while the tattoo was being inked in and the pattern of the tattoo itself could be significant. She leaned down and sniffed the tattoo. A slight smell of rot. She used the Uni-Mind and consulted Lady Lessa's photo and vid collection again. She was looking for a shot of her bare left shoulder to see if the tattoo had been there previously.

There—a set of shots of her splashing in the aqua waters of Bazz wearing a colorful swimsuit.

No tattoo.

Stenibelle went over her with her arcane kit of holystones and various other detectors. She was found to not have been to the astral plane, nor had she been exposed to any of the more obvious ingredients used in arcane rituals. She did not read as a magical creature herself.

But, Stenibelle's Shadow tech detector went utterly wild, so much so it cracked in her hand. This poor woman was saturated in Shadow tech, and probably more than enough to be rendered fatally toxic. Predictably, the Shadow tech came from the tattoo on her left shoulder.

What had Morgan-Jeterix said—that the *George Parr* had been befouled with Shadow tech, and here it was, slowly killing this girl.

The Uni-Mind jumped back into her coat. So, there it was, this woman, and possibly the most of the regular crew with her, were bespelled.

She grappled with herself for a moment. What to do? She needed the Cammara data, but this poor crewman required assisting. What could she do? She wasn't a Hospitaler and her knowledge of Shadow tech was minimal at best. If she attempted to treat Lady Lessa and got it wrong she could end up killing her. And, what about the rest of them down in the hold? She was only one person. She couldn't watch over them all.

Time was wasting.

"I know! I'll get the data, and once I have it, I can use it to ask

Professor Shurlamp for assistance. I'll refuse to give it to her unless she relents. She might know what to do, or, she could recommend a wise course of action. She could get help."

That seemed the best plan: get the data as quickly as possible and then force Professor Shurlamp to do something, anything for the crew.

Leaving Lady Lessa wrapped up in her robe on the bed, Stenibelle exited the room and tricked the lock so she could re-enter without having to pick it. She snuck away down the empty corridor, the Ceril-Cone data steadily ratcheting through her brain.

Captain Duval: Deck 2, Officer's Wing, accessible via the Executive Lift at Junction 4.

She moved down the long corridor knowing exactly where she needed to go. Junction 4 will be, from her current position, two hundred feet forward. There were many lifts dotting the deck, but only three went to the bridge and only one went to the Officer's Wing.

This one, right here: the Executive Lift, its doors innocently clamshelled shut. There was a palm lock, keeping the riff-raff out. The Ceril hammered away information.

Use access door L-76 to enter the lift shaft and climb up.

She found the panel and opened it, revealing a small maintenance crawl way leading into the yawning open space of the lift shaft. A locked grate barred her entrance. It was a magneto lock requiring a hydraulic key and was un-networked. She could pick it and nobody on the bridge would know a thing, though the lock would require more force than a human pair of hands could manage, even with the Gift of Strength. Out came her VUNKULA, the battle club opened and latched on. After just a few moments of work she had it twisted open. She squirmed in and was soon climbing the rungs upward toward Deck 2, the VUNKULA clamping on tight with a metal deforming CLANK, hauling her up fast.

As she neared Deck 3, the abandoned silence of the ship was lost, replaced with a frenetic howl of noise. Rough, beatless music highlighted with a pervasive cloud of moans and aggressive chatter drifted through the lift door, mixed with the delicate crystalline tinkling of glass breaking and loose items being tossed about. As she passed Deck 3, she smelled the acrid notes of cigarette and menthol smoke, the harsh cheap kind from Bazz. She also smelled the lurking galling stench of urine and the flat, tired aroma of stale beer soaked in carpeting.

It was as if the entire ship was abandoned, except for Deck 3 which was densely populated by barbarians having a rave. Deck 3 Forward, per the Ceril, was for officers and heads of section. What were the officers doing?? The access panel was there nearby, she decided to take a quick peek. Pushing through into the brightly lit hallway, a dismal scene unfolded before her. There was rubbish tossed about, empty bottles, crumpled papers, half-eaten meals and other flotsam. The walls were gouged, graffiti was painted. People rolled about in drunken and Kooked-Up stupors. As with the ghoulish man in the hold, these were all filthy and nightmarish personages dressed in Fleet uniforms. There were shifty, horrid men and painted, teased-up women, barbed and pierced, some with 4-D tattoos pointing at their privates and flashing. None of the lot registered in her Ceril-data: it was quiet, giving her some momentary privacy with her own thoughts. The regular crew was replaced with a pack of filthy disreputables for reasons unknown. She had no idea how or why such a thing could have happened. She pulled back into the lift shaft and continued upward.

She reached Deck 2, skirting around the Lift Car that was suspended there. She found the maintenance crawl, faded into the Shadows, and squeezed in to the environs of Deck 2. In contrast to the lower decks which were rather utilitarian, it was quite opulent: fine wood paneling all around, corniced framing and expensive Hoban tiles lined the floor. A gallery of fine oil paintings depicting the busts of majestic, well-dressed, unsmiling people wigged in the Remnath fashion were lit by golden lamps. Subdued Remnath stringed music played over the intercom, drowning out all hint of the barbarism going on below on Deck 3.

The Ceril was back, slapping her in the sinuses, load-packing her mind with information. She drifted in and went to the Captain's door. She heard notes of quiet conversation within.

She rapped on the door, hoping he would answer and she could drift in. Time to come face to face with this fellow.

The talking within ceased. A moment later the door swung open a crack. "Who's there?" came a voice. The door opened fully and a tall woman came out with dark blue hair. She looked up and down the corridor, perplexed. "Who's there?" she asked again in an accented voice.

More Ceril-Cone information assaulted her head-space: Lt. Remm Deckard, first officer and graduate of Traveler school for women. Her birthplace was listed as: Deckard Continent, Planet Fall, however Professor Shurlamp disputed that. The Professor's Ceril information stated instead that Deckard was a Famora from Moedron, a hellish place if ever there was one and that she was extremely dangerous.

Dangerous?

Her appearance didn't betray anything of the sort. She was tall and pretty with a stately face, her blue hair pulled back and tied. She was wearing a Full Fleet uniform, dark blue coat, frilly white shirt, pants and deep Falloon boots. Quite a bit different from the more lady-like Tremblar uniform Gwendolyn wore. Her hands emerging from the frills and felt were delicate and feminine.

Steeling her nerves, Stenibelle drifted past her and entered the room as the woman closed the door behind her.

Success, she was in.

The room inside was equally as luxurious as the corridor. The far wall was rim-shot with windows looking out on the starry night of open space studded with panning light cones from the sensing nodes of the ship. Grand couches and fine wood tables were arranged in the interior of the room astride rugs and rich carpets. Trays of biscuits, cheeses and porcelain pots steaming with scented tea and coffee sat on the tables.

Tea and coffee, very cultured and reasonable, unlike the spilt beer and cigarette stench down below.

Centered on the interior wall was a full-length framed portrait depicting a turbid black scene. Layers upon layers of black, it looked like Shadow tech to Stenibelle. Standing in the center of the Shadow tech was a tall, slender female wearing a tight-fitting black costume, like an oilskin. The figure was wearing a spherical helmet of some sort with the front portion of the sphere cut away revealing her face. She had a fair face with sharp, pencil-like features. Over her eyes, she wore a protruding pair of brass or gold geared goggles. She also wore a great cape that seemed to also be made of Shadow tech. The painting was oddly lurid and disquieting. Things seemed to move. The woman's goggled eyes seemed to follow her.

Two men were sitting at couches in the center of the room. One was slim, tallish fellow in a tailored Fleet uniform brimming with ivy and stars. He had a sallow face and light blonde hair mixed with wisps of thoughtful Remnath gray.

Ceril-Cone tele-type flash wired across her thoughts and embossed themselves. She'd never met the man before, but she knew exactly who he was: Captain Duval, Lord of Wilshire from the Wiln area of Remnath. The information Hannah-Ben Shurlamp had given her were complete, both the good and the bad.

Captain Duval.

4th Lord Wilshire of the current line.

A Fleet captain in his tenth appointment to the chair of the George Parr

Child prodigy with the oboe.

Studied political science at the University of Mercia. Was a first-rate brandtball player—winger position.

Hero of the Battle of Sorrander-Quo.

Society man, married to a debutante from Falz, his second wife.

Programmability: Allendi

Churchgoer

Frequent donator to charitable causes.

Anarchist.

Murdered a man once for a minor slight and hid his body.

Frequent adulterer, especially with his first officer, Lt. Remm Deckard.

Trafficker in women and children and human flesh.

Member of the Nillists of Punt: Stated goal, destruction of the universe.

A churchgoer and murderer who would see the end of all things, and here he was, right in front of her, drinking tea on a couch.

The man sitting across from him reminded Stenibelle of a pig. At first glance he seemed rather handsome and striking, but it faded quickly. He had a round, unappealing face, a small blunt nose and wore a black suit of odd manufacture. She too knew exactly who he was: Rodrigo of Burgon, a Xaphan Warlord sitting in comfort aboard a Fleet ship, an offense that would have Captain Duval off his chair and firmly in prison should it ever come out. His face was on the Xaphan Wall back at the Fleet, granting permission for any personnel to assassinate him without question.

Rodrigo of Burgon drank from a cup of tea that he regularly enhanced with a thick dark red liquid poured from a flask.

Hannah-Ben Shurlamp had a wealth of information on him as well, pounded out in blaring Ceril information.

Xaphan Warlord from Miaas and titular head of the court of Burgon.

Occasional lover of Camilla of Sorrander, another infamous Xaphan potentate.

Suspected of cannibalism—confirmed by the professor's information.

Suspected Xaphan Cabalist again confirmed.

Nillist of Punt.

Sitting next to Burgon was a slender woman wearing a dark cranberry robe printed with tiny, colorful flowers. Her long legs and feet were bare, tucked up underneath her waist.

Is she wearing any knickers? Stenibelle wondered. It didn't look like it.

Her fawn-colored hair, shiny and well-tended, was pulled back from her face and held in place with several jeweled combs. A sequined headband ran across her forehead. She sat perfectly still, eyes closed, as if in a deep trance, the rise and fall of her breast nearly imperceptible. Stenibelle guessed if she stood up, this woman, even shoeless, would be of exceptional height, much taller than herself or even Gwendolyn.

She held her right hand to her breast, fingers contorted into an uncomfortable bent/extended position. Her left hand was stretched out toward Burgon's, the pads of her fingers lightly touching and breezing across his wrist in a minute but hypnotic pattern. Burgon's wrist and arm reacted slightly to her touches, goosing-up, his sinews pulling taught like a lute string, plucked into slow passion by them.

Stenibelle received additional Ceril-Cone information:

Melazarr of Caroline. 25th daughter in the court of Wilhelmina. She had one father and ten mothers—the Xaphan custom of gene splicing from a number of donors was practiced often on Caroline. She had inherited familial Giantism as was common with the Carolines and her height was listed as 77 beltegues, or, in League terms, 7'1. Her weight, a whopping three hundred pounds.

Three hundred pounds?? Stenibelle marveled. Melazarr was long and skinny. The weight must all be bone and muscle.

More information.

A Xaphan Tropist capable of inducing pleasure with the slightest touch and bound to the Court of Burgon for the last twenty years.

And, according to A-Ram and Alesta, she was an Extra-Planar entity known as a *Merten*, possessing the critical data she needed.

There she was. Now to get at the data.

Around her droll conversation unfolded.

"Who was at the door?" Captain Duval asked.

"Nobody was there, the corridor was empty," Remm Deckard replied, resuming her seat.

"I distinctly heard a knock."

"As did I," Rodrigo said. "Probably one of those barley-coated knockabouts you have manning the ship. Had I known of your pressing need for manpower, I'd have brought my own hand-picked crew."

Remm Deckard turned a slight shade of red. "Ha! A bunch of Xaphans manning a Fleet Sprint ship. That shall be a bad day indeed."

Duval interjected. "I determine who is placed at key positions on my ship, dear Burgon, let us not forget that. These people have their uses, and, when that time has passed, they shall suffer the same fate as those who preceded them. None shall be missed, I assure you."

"Not the women. We need the women," Burgon replied.

"Yes, quite." Duval took a sip of his tea and stared at the ominous painting hanging on the wall. "So, what news? I am eager to get underway. I shall sneak out of the League and return a Destroyer with the Shadow tech Goddess at my side, wiping clean this place and remaking it as I see fit."

Burgon became annoyed. "How many times must I tell you? This process takes time."

Remm Deckard was skeptical. "Time we don't have, Burgon. We could be boarded by the Fleet for inspections, summoned by an Admiral or compelled away on some errant quest. We cannot hide what we have done here forever. I thought we would be out of the League by now. You boasted we would be."

Burgon retorted. "Just a little more time. The women you have given me are weak in Shadow tech, like a basket full of turnips. Good Xaphan women are much better at yielding Shadow tech. Once we have enough, we will know the location of Cammara and we may begin our quest."

"And these people on Cammara can open the way to the Shadow tech Goddess at last?"

Cammara!! Stenibelle moved into position and listened.

"Indeed," Rodrigo said in a dreamy voice. "Golden Cammara. Immortal Cammara. There we can sit back in luxury and watch as all else is destroyed. There, we shall be masters of a new, properly-conceived universe. These are the End of Times we have strived for at long last, dear Captain. Let us head into Xaphan space and steal us some women there. They shall yield much faster."

"Unfortunately we are a Fleet ship and cannot just go into Xaphan space without due cause. And, there's also the small matter of your friend, Camilla of Sorrander, wanting to stick your head out on the mast of her ship."

Burgon turned an angry shade of red. "Yes, thank you for reminding me."

Remm Deckard pointed at the silent Melazarr of Caroline. "What about her? She's a Xaphan, right? Why don't we sacrifice her?"

"Because, she is my personal Tropist," Burgon replied. Melazarr's fingers stabbed him into bliss and his voice strained. ". . . *And I need her*."

"How much more Shadow tech do you need?" Remm Deckard asked. "We're running out of crew."

"Then get me more. Many more. My casks must be overflowing."

Duval set his cup down. "My dear Burgon, this isn't Xaphan space. Here in the League when reputable people turn up missing they are indeed missed, unlike the disposable K-List trash I have manning the ship now. Questions are asked, investigations are launched. But, have no fear, more victims will soon be available. We'll have them by tomorrow."

"I shall wish to inspect them," Burgon said. "We cannot harvest quality Shadow tech without victims of proper stock."

Duval shrugged. "If you must. I'll have my First take you down to the hold and you may inspect those we capture for yourself."

"No, no, I don't trust your witch from Moedron. She'll probably attempt to assassinate me along the way. You take me, Captain."

Remm Deckard seethed and pulled a horrid, ugly knife from the interior of her coat. "Would I do such a thing, man of Burgon?"

Rodrigo yawned and pointed at an odd black box sitting near the windows. It looked like a large bird cage paneled shut with slats of wood and tarred black. The box rattled a little, it seemed to smoke. "Careful,

woman. One word from my lips, and my Trempalar Box will open, and
you shall bear witness to the horrid wonders of Midas. It is my personal
protection that I carry and it has served me well in the past, I assure you."

Deckard glanced at the box and hesitated. "I don't think anything's
in there."

"Care to find out?"

Duval scowled. "Enough! And I could, at a word, flood this entire
deck in V-Trax gas and have you and your Tropist whore incapacitated
in seconds. Let us compose ourselves for now and be reasonable, there
shall be a fitting time for chaos in the days to come."

V-Trax. Another sickening wave of Ceril hit Stenibelle hard.

V-Trax was an old Fleet tactic used by ship captains who didn't trust
their crews and were in fear for their lives. They would pump in a
poisonous gas known as *Varensus Traxsafona* in select areas of the ship,
usually the bridge or their personal quarters. This gas was deadly to any
not having been administered the antidote.

Another variable she had to consider.

Melazarr's fingers quickened their pace. Burgon covered his mouth
and groaned slightly.

There she was, Melazarr of Caroline, the key to Stenibelle's mission,
the shield that would save her House and she couldn't get to her with
these cretins about. It was maddening. She had to do something. The
little piece of her psyche that was still Bunged-Up spoke with brutal
clarity.

Just kill the three of them and be done with it.

Kill them? She supposed these three deserved it to some extent, after
all they were colluding to bring about the end of the universe. But, how
to do it? Stenibelle, despite her skills and arcane equipment, was no
warrior. Her best advantage was stealth and surprise. She could probably
kill one of them with her Grenville 40, or with her VUNKULA, but what
about the other two? The Captain was armed with a standard MiMs
pistol, a very small caliber weapon but still lethal, and he could order the
deck gassed with V-Trax poison on command. Burgon was a Xaphan
Warlord, he must have considerable martial skills at his disposal, and he
had his arcane Trempalar Box which was intended to protect him from
attack. And what about Remm Deckard? Her Ceril information listed her

as *Extremely Dangerous*. What did that mean? Was she a warrior? Was she an assassin? Her capabilities were unknown. Stenibelle could kill one of them but then have to deal with the other two. And, what about Melazarr herself? Would she be compliant? Would she cooperate? Would she be hostile? She was obviously drugged or in a deep trance, that would complicate matters as well. A seven foot tall, three hundred pound female would be quite a handful.

And then there were the crew, or what was left of them in the hold. Eliminating the Captain or the First Officer might trigger some sort of reprisal from the people on the bridge. They might panic and try to flee the League. They could jettison the crew or burn them or do any number of things.

Given all this, killing them outright didn't seem a practical option. She had to maintain her stealth, remain unseen. She decided to disable them and try to get Melazarr away from the area so she could figure out how to get the information out of her.

Stenibelle noticed a fresh pot of tea brewing on a burner, the sweet fragrance of plums and blueberries drifting out. A thought crossed her head.

Stenibelle pulled an ochre Holystone from the depths of her HRN. The ochre Holystone had been invented by her sister Virginia of all people. Her husband, Maximillian of Pole, sometimes had issues sleeping after eating too much of her wonderful cooking—he had a tender stomach and a tendency to bloat. The ochre Holystone, full of herbs and stalks of select plants, was intended to settle the stomach, clear the bowels and provide a sweet feeling of indifference. Virginia was never a great herbalist, and her ochre Holystone worked a little too well, often making the user prone to flatulence and drunk with indifferent bliss, eventually passing out. She took three ochres, all she had, and silently dropped them into the tea. Then, she backed away and waited. She had to be careful, as the fumes alone could lighten her head and dull her senses as well. She had to remain sharp.

After a while, Burgon had finished his cup. "Woman!" he said to Remm Deckard. "I would like some more tea!" He held out his cup. "Would you be so kind?"

"Let your bitch over there do it."

"She is royalty. You are a League peasant."

Deckard stood up and seethed. "Captain, may I show him a few things about myself? I'm dying to . . ." The room seemed to get a little hotter.

Duval laughed and stood up. He took Burgon's cup. "Please be seated, Lt., I'll get it." He went to the tea service and poured three fresh cups. Stenibelle sucked in her breath and watched. She could smell the slightly cloying scent of the dissolved ochres in the tea. She would have to observe carefully and spring when the time was ripe. She covered her mouth with her hand to avoid breathing in the fumes as much as possible.

It shouldn't be long. Three ochres should fire them right up.

Duval returned to the table and they began drinking the tainted tea, all except for Melazarr of Caroline who remained in a lock-still trance.

"I was inspecting the hold," Burgon said. "There are plenty of crew ready to be harvested." He slurped his tea. "The cargo is full of them."

"Those in Hold 1 are individuals who have family in influential positions, who donate money to the Fleet with frequency, and, who often enquire about their children under my command. We need them alive for now in case one comes calling."

Burgon finished his tea and poured himself more. "Such civilities are obsolete in these times, Captain. Their families are inconsequential as are your quaint efforts at maintaining appearances. Such considerations have no meaning at the end of all things."

Duval took a drink. "Yes, well, until we actually see some sort of results, I shall outwardly maintain the status quo and be an apparently loyal captain in the Fleet. Until the time has come to unleash Hell, I shall be a citizen of Heaven in good standing."

Remm Deckard stood up and removed her Fleet coat. She fanned her face with her hand. A hot, flushed sensation—that was one of the symptoms that the ochre was taking effect. It shouldn't be long now.

Stenibelle was feeling a tad hot herself. The room spun a little. The fumes were seeping into her head.

"Is it getting hot in here?" Duval asked. "If the engineer was still with us I'd give him an earful."

As they drank their tea, the Com rang in. "Sir, long range scans indicate a Xaphan freighter coming in, 6:22am of 8:19pm. She's riding in the Gillman Slot to avoid standard Fleet detection."

Duval motioned for Remm Deckard to come in and she did. She unbuttoned his collar.

"Compliment?" Duval asked as he unbuttoned her pants.

A gross reduction in inhibition—yet another ochre trait. Stenibelle recalled the normally shy Virginia running nude through the gardens after an ochre session. The wet sounds of passionate kisses filtered up.

"Unknown. It appears to be a shipload of refugees, possibly from Woodward."

"Understood. File a . . . false flight plan to the Fleet, make our heading the Hedgepeth under the pretense of investigating suspected . . . Xaphan traffic there. Meanwhile, send to navigation and plot solution to intercept the vessel down the Gillman Slot, full communications blackout procedures in place. Send to helm, make sail, best possible speed. Time to intercept?"

"At full sail, three hours."

"Excellent." He groaned a little. "Keep me advised."

He turned to Rodrigo as Remm Deckard licked his neck. "See, dear Burgon, something always presents itself. An unregistered Xaphan transport just crying out for our attention is en route."

"And you have no fear of the Fleet?"

Duval scoffed. "'Course not. We're all one big happy group, are we not? We just filed a flight plan stating we shall be in the Hedgepeth, therefore where else would we be? No one is checking, for Creation's sake, and with the speed of this class of ship, once we finish we'll be there in no time for verisimilitude's sake."

"As a matter of interest, dear Captain, what will you do once you intercept this unfortunate craft?"

"Quite simple. We approach. We jam. We disable. We board. We take the women. We space the men. We destroy the ship using our custom-mounted Xaphan cassagrain beams to make it appear as an enemy raiding action."

Remm Deckard unbuttoned her shirt and removed her pants. She straddled Duval and soon they were copulating right in front of Rodrigo, who watched with fury. He stumbled in and tried to insert himself into the situation. The three of them had faded into a squirming primal situation with Rodrigo a pawing third wheel trying to work his way in. They became consumed with their passions.

It was time.

Her head feeling a bit numb, Stenibelle got close to Melazarr.

Melazarr's eyes snapped open and stared at her though Stenibelle was still faded into the shadows. Her eyes were the most amazing color— yellowish-brown flecked with gold, like a lion's eye and she smelled like a baked dessert.

Melazarr struggled to speak. "Muh, muh . . ." Stenibelle could smell herbs and tinctures on her breath. Burgon had her drugged with something potent.

Stenibelle took Melazarr by the hands. Melazarr slid off the couch and stood up, her feet slapping on the tiles. She towered over Stenibelle. So far she seemed compliant, in a drugged, child-like sort of manner.

Her goal was to get Melazarr out of the room, off Deck 2 and somewhere deep into the ship where the coordinates to Cammara could be extracted in privacy. She led her away to the door, Melazarr teetering a bit on the balls of her feet. It was tough sledding with Melazarr's weight. It was like trying to move a block of iron around.

"Muh, muh . . ." she stammered. She leaned into Stenibelle, putting her arms around her, grabbing her, trying to get at her wrist.

"No, no . . . Shhhhhh, shhhhhhhh," Stenibelle said, trying to keep her quiet. As Melazarr pawed at her, she tried the door and it was locked. Stenibelle couldn't turn the latch, it seemed to be frozen in place. She produced her lock picks and went to work on the door. The lock wouldn't budge. She didn't understand, why couldn't she get through? She sweated and felt confused, the fumes from the ochres were definitely affecting her as well. She was having trouble seeing properly.

Why won't the damn door open?

Melazarr would not leave her alone, pawing and grabbing. Stenibelle took her by the hands and lead her a few paces away. "Sit here, please," she said. Melazarr seated her herself on the floor, her long legs stretching out in front of her. Stenibelle noticed Melazarr had a deep, ugly burn mark on her right shoulder blade. It was seared into her flesh, as if from a branding iron.

Stenibelle set back to work. The damn lock still wouldn't budge. Stenibelle had never had issues like this with a lock before. What was the matter?

Wait a moment!! What had she been thinking? She had her trusty brown Holystones. She could get both herself and Melazarr out of the ship right now and be gone to the safety of Planet Fall. Once there she could figure out how to extract the coordinates and then go to Professor Shurlamp or Lt. Gwendolyn and inform her of the doings on this ship and that the crew needed helping. Lt. Gwendolyn would take action. Lt. Gwendolyn would save the crew. Why hadn't she thought of it before?

The fumes, they were certainly messing her up.

She reached into her pockets to fetch them. She slapped at her HRN. "Where in Creation are my Holystones?" she cried.

They were missing from their pockets.

She glanced at Melazarr. Scattered all around her on the floor were various items from her HRN: arcane danger detectors, papers, small boxes. (For the Love of Creation there was Professor Shurlamp's Uni-Mind) and, like a collection of gumballs, were most of her Holystones.

Melazarr had effortlessly picked her pockets and emptied their contents to the floor like a master cut-purse.

"Gods, Melazarr, what have you done?" Stenibelle scrambled and fitfully returned the items to her HRN. She reached for the Uni-Mind but Melazarr snatched it away.

"Muh, muh, muh . . ." she grunted.

Stenibelle had several Holystones in her hands, but she was having issues distinguishing color, yet another effect of the ochres. Which ones were the brown ones? She couldn't determine the browns from the reds from the greens and purples. They were fuzzy in her hand.

Never mind. Take Melazarr and flee! Get that door open! Shoot the doorknob off if you have to! Quit the ship later when her head had cleared.

To her bewilderment, the Uni-Mind sat before Melazarr between her legs. Somehow, she had accessed its holo-desk. A lurid holographic keyboard hovered in front of her, complete with slides, glyphs and side controllers. Melazarr was typing away at fast speed, her long fingers a blur. She wasn't even looking at what she was doing, she was just keying in data, her fingers moving on their own. Lit up in holographics a complex star chart was forming before Stenibelle's eyes, coming together in 3-D complexity complete with vectors, lines of force, AM/PM compass headings, planetary systems, nebular anomalies, and notable stars/stellar bodies.

"Muh, muh , map to Ca—Cammara," she stammered, a dazed grin on her face.

Stenibelle was astounded. On her own, Melazarr was yielding the information both she and Rodrigo of Burgon so desperately needed. She watched her work.

The Merten will give the information to you, A-Ram had said.

The chart was nearly complete.

"Melazarr!!"

Just then, Rodrigo of Burgon seized Melazarr by the hair, roughly pulling her away. Like a scurrying spider, the Uni-Mind closed up and headed back to Stenibelle at a run with its cargo of fresh data. It scurried up her leg and vanished into the depths of her coat. Grunting, Burgon and Melazarr spun round and round.

"Dance with me, Mel!!" he cried. His pants fell to his ankles, Melazarr's robe came away and they began having sex, Melazarr much bigger than Burgon.

"Sir," came the Com. "Captain Duval? We are detecting high levels of noxious gas in your quarters. Sir, are you all right?"

The bridge crew had detected the vapors of her ochre Holystones. Things were falling apart.

"We're sending a team to check on you."

The bridge crew were proceeding. Duval, Deckard, Rodrigo and Melazarr weren't listening, they were deep into their orgy, everybody pounding away. Melazarr, on all fours, continued to stare at Stenibelle. "Muh, muh . . ." she repeated as Burgon hammered her into the floor.

Frustrated, she scooped up as many Holystones as she could, leaving a few rolling about. She tried the door one more time, and, to her shock, it opened easily. Why couldn't she get it open before? She didn't have time to ponder. She exited just as the team from the bridge arrived and piled into the room.

9—Saving the *George Parr*

Stenibelle returned to Lady Lessa's room, her head clearing.

Lessa was still out cold, wrapped up in her robe, which was good; though, the rate at which she took breath seemed somewhat accelerated and more ragged than before, as if she'd just run up a flight of stairs. Her temperature also seemed to be on the rise. The room was quite cold, yet she was burning up. Stenibelle pulled the covers back and loosened her robe. Clearly, her condition was worsening and, as Burgon had said, the crew was being used as some sort of sacrifice. The only reason she was still alive was her House of Walpole from Onaris was just influential enough to afford her a bit of protection. The notion of murdering his entire crew hadn't seemed to bother Duval one little bit, neither had the thought of the entire Universe ending as well. The man and his First Officer were certainly insane.

A few strands of Lessa's hair got caught on Stenibelle's sleeve. The strands came off her scalp without resistance. This woman was quickly fading.

She could feel the Uni-Mind jostling about deep within her HRN. Full of data, it was like a living thing eager to share its treasure trove of knowledge with its master, Hannah-Ben Shurlamp on far away Kana. Stenibelle went to the terminal and fired it up. The Uni-Mind came out of her HRN and took immediate control of the terminal. Screens flashed by at impossible speeds, information was shared and pathways established.

As the Uni-Mind worked, she took stock of her things that Melazarr had stolen. Her Grenville 40 was still there, but not her Hertamer heat gun. She was missing a few of her arcane detectors, but those could be replaced. She sorted through her Holystones, those were the key to her escape. She sorted them out and, to her relief, there were the three Brown ones mixed in with the rest—her salvation. She quickly returned them to their proper place in her HRN.

The Uni-Mind was successful and the terminal cone settled and took shape. An ornate study appeared, a smaller one than previous. It was dark and shut down, her fine desk unoccupied. Her wand-like glyph sat neatly on her blotter like a gnarled stick. After several minutes a pool of dim light spilled across the floor and up the padded ruby walls. Stenibelle watched the slender, well-made form of a woman in a fine pinkish robe and a pair of silk slippers make her way across the room to the desk. The figure kept a demure hand at her breast keeping her robe shut. Stenibelle assumed it was Professor Shurlamp; the figure lacked her usual snowy white gown and towering wig. Checking her time piece, it was the middle of the night in Calvert on Kana—Professor Shurlamp had been roused from her bed. Stenibelle also noted her robed body was perfect: well-proportioned bosom, hour-glass waist and hips, slender arms and legs, sucked-in stomach—Professor Shurlamp was apparently quite the looker. That weird little guy she was married to had scored in a big way with a wife like that. Her thick head of raven black hair flowed over her shoulders and back with a slight curl. Her unpowdered skin was olive-like and swarthy. Unwigged, unpowdered, it was like seeing a totally different person.

She seated herself at her desk and there could be no question that the dark, raven person with the beautiful body sitting there was Professor Shurlamp. Her grace of line and perfect lady-like posture was unmistakable. And there were her roving brown eyes, seeing everything. "Good morning, Lady Stenibelle," she said in her usual authoritarian manner. "What news?"

"Good morning, Professor. I'm sorry to have woken you. I don't have the data yet, but I know where it is. I have additional questions and concerns."

She picked up her glyph and several screens appeared around Shurlamp's head revealing a bewildering amount of information reflected on her swarthy face. "No data? The Uni-Mind is reporting a data collection recently. Let us have a look, shall we?"

Charts and data that Melazarr had created appeared in front of her in lurid red lines. She focused in on the data. "What is this? Where did you collect this?"

"From Burgon."

"I see. According to this data we utilize the geographic center of Kana as a starting point of reference and look to the constellation Orestes . . . the star Bizzum in the left quadrant . . . two minutes south by west and note the occluded binary star . . . ."

"Professor?"

She didn't answer. She was engrossed in the moment of discovery. She moved the star chart around with her Glyph, following the directions given. She spoke out loud, ". . . and take a compass bearing Z azimuth, tan minus sin L. 47 degrees right ascension, and . . . ."

She looked around. "Where is the rest? The data are not complete."

"I was interrupted."

"And you collected this data from Burgon?"

"No, from Melazarr of Caroline, his Tropist."

Professor Shurlamp was uncharacteristically puzzled. "His Tropist had the data?"

"Yes. She input the data into the Uni-Mind. I tried to get her out of the room to safety, but I couldn't get the door open. It was locked tight and I couldn't pick it. I've never seen anything like it before."

"Rodrigo of Burgon is a Xaphan warlord, and, Melazarr of Caroline is his Tropist, he undoubtedly has her branded with a Chastity Key. That is a common Xaphan practice. They are very easy to install and very difficult to defeat. She cannot venture far from him without the doors locking tight. It insures she is never far from his side and cannot escape. It is a lot of Cabalist nonsense."

"It works, Professor. The door was not budging."

"I must have the rest of the data. What I see here looks promising, it looks correct. I must have the rest. When can you get it?"

"I need Melazarr alone, then I'll have the rest. For now I need your help, it is of the utmost importance."

The Professor composed herself. "What? Ask. I am yours."

"The Captain, his First, and this Rodrigo of Burgon spoke of the end of the Universe."

"As I said before, they are Nillists of Punt and that is their stated goal. It is simply idle talk."

"No, no, Professor. They mentioned someone called the Shadow tech Goddess, and on Cammara they may gain access to her. It didn't seem like idle talk to them. I must admit, I'm extremely concerned."

"And why is that, Lady Stenibelle? That the Captain and Rodrigo of Burgon were discussing frightening things in private? That same Rodrigo of Burgon who has disenfranchised himself with every Xaphan Household across their territory to such extent that Camilla of Sorrander and several others are actively seeking his head. The same Rodrigo of Burgon who has bankrupted his court and now seeks pliable, willing and wealthy followers in League space to entertain his madness? I suggest you concentrate your efforts on Burgon's Tropist for the time being."

"But, what about the crew? The captain has them in some sort of stasis. The crew are very sick and in need of helping."

"Your task is to collect the data for Cammara. Your concern for the crew is admirable, however misplaced. Think to yourself and consider the rebirth of your Household. And, at the moment, you've more pressing things to consider."

"I do?"

"The Com Officer on the bridge has noted our communication activity and a detail has been dispatched to investigate. They shall be arriving any moment."

Stenibelle looked about in a panic.

"Stay alert, Lady Stenibelle. I shall expect to hear from you again when you have the rest of the data. I will do what I can to assist you from here."

"Can you inform the Fleet? Can you . . ."

And with that, the Professor vanished. The Uni-Mind buttoned up and she returned it to its pocket.

Someone arrived outside and pounded on the door. "Who's in there?" came a voice from the other side of the door. "Open up!"

She opened the closet door to hide Lady Lessa's body. She accidentally stepped into her camera, activating it. It puttered to life and floated up to eye-level. It was an expensive, complicated camera, made for somebody with a love of photography. It floated over to Lessa's prostrate body and waited there for her to command it.

More pounding on the door, the lock being tried. No time!

"We're coming in!" came the gruff voice from outside.

She faded into the shadows just as the door opened and readied her VUNKULA, dipping it into a compartment full of sleeping powder. Two people entered a moment later, a man and a woman, bridge crew apparently. As before, they didn't look like typical clean-cut Fleet crew, they looked like shifty vagabonds in rumpled uniforms that evaded her Ceril information, it was blissfully silent. The man had a stubbly shaved head, the woman had a dyed shock of bright pink hair, twisted into rings. Her nose was pierced, her lips were painted black. A garish 4D tattoo of an arrow lit up in neon lights blinked off and on, pointing at her crotch. She held a Dare heat gun up to level.

They walked in and noted the active terminal. Lady Lessa's camera floated there, looking for attention like a mechanical hovering dog.

"Frame?" it asked in a hopeful manner.

"It's her camera," he said. "It must be malfunctioning."

The woman walked past Stenibelle, went to the bed and leaned over Lady Lessa. "How'd she get in here? How'd she get out of her tube?"

"I've seen a couple of 'em get out and blunder around. I caught one myself the other day and was under orders to take her down to the hold. Bad luck for her I guess."

"So she got out of her tube, stumbled in here, accessed her camera and made a Com to Hoban and then got in bed? I don't think so. Stumbling around's one thing, doing complex tasks is another." She looked Lessa over and quickly discovered the pinkie in her hand. "What's this?" She picked it up for a moment and quickly discovered its narcotic properties. She dropped it.

"What is it?" the male asked.

"Some sort of stunning device, I don't know. I could feel its effects taking hold as I picked it up. Don't touch it, it's very potent."

The male accessed the terminal. The stern blue-haired face of Lt. Remm Deckard appeared. "What is your situation?" she asked.

"We've discovered an activated float camera. We found the crewman in her bed clutching a device that appears to render one unconscious."

"Not possible. We've an intruder aboard. Very well. Take her down to the hold. Then commence an immediate search of the ship for the intruder."

"Aye." The male crewman ended the Com. "You heard her. Come on, let's go. She's going to the front of the line."

"I'm for just burning the room up with her in it and saying she resisted. I don't want to go down to the hold." The female checked the settings of her Dare heat gun and adjusted it.

"Sure, sure, whatever. Let's go, it's freezing in here."

Lessa groaned and thrashed. Her skin was bright pink, she was burning up with fever. Probably wouldn't last long. Her Floating camera hovered near her bedside.

"Frame?" it asked, again. "Frame?" It displayed a cone of photos from her trips to Bazz with her friends. Bright sun, smiling faces full of possibilities. Young love in full blossom . . . and here she was, prostrate, burning, her Shadow tech contaminated body wrapped up in a terrycloth robe. Her hair falling out.

The male crewman dashed the camera into the wall, all the color and light going out. The pink-haired female grinned, her teeth accented by her black lips.

"Bye, bye, babe . . ."

Stenibelle closed her eyes and made her decision. She couldn't leave Lessa to her unsavory fate. She had to try to help her—certainly that's what her male counterparts would do, and even if that weren't the case, what did it matter?

That's what she would do.

And, unlike the situation on Deck 2, these crew here didn't look to be highly skilled assassins, war heroes or Xaphan Warlords. They looked like two punks dredged out of the trash, and they were standing right next to each other.

Stenibelle struck. She extended her VUNKULA and slammed the door shut, startling both of the crewmen. She shook her hands and produced three green Holystones. She threw all three of them, hopelessly burying both crewmen in a tangled clog of webbing. She could hear the crewmen struggling deep within the tangle, hopelessly snared. "You're right," Stenibelle said. "There is an intruder on-board—me!"

"I have a weapon!" the female crewman yelled, her voice somewhat muffled by the webbing. "I'll use it!"

"A heat gun? And do what with it? You'll burn yourself in the process. I've a few questions, and you are going to answer them!"

"We'll not say a thing!"

"Then I'll torture you first, then kill. Do you think I won't?"

She uncoiled her VUNKULA, dipping it into a series of pockets, coating it with powder and salve. She then let it out and worked it into the depths of the webbing, poking and prodding, searching for the two crewmen. She felt it hit the soft flesh of one of the crewmen buried deep, and she gave them a good stab.

"Ouch!!" the female cried. "What are you doing?"

She repeated the process, this time locating the male crewman and stabbed him too. He cursed in pain. Stenibelle waited a few minutes to let the cocktails of narcotics and hallucinogens go to work.

Now, what to terrify them with? Stenibelle thought and thought. She recalled once scaring her sister Lucile half to death with a handful of bugs she'd found outside in a tree.

"Lucile . . . look what I've got for you . . ."

"EEEEEEEE!! Ohmygosh!! Take those away, Bel, before I tell Mother! What is wrong with you?"

Stenibelle began. "Can you feel the insects, burrowing their way through the webbing to reach your warm flesh?" she asked, planting the seeds of horror, filling them with terror. "Do you hear the crunching and popping? Do you feel them burrowing into your flesh to get to the sweet fat underneath?"

She listened to the panicked groans and grunts of the trapped crewman. They rustled about, trying to get free. "Uh . . . uh . . . I hear them! I hear them chewing through the webbing. I—"

"Yes," Stenibelle said, being as diabolically creative as she could, "First, they will bore into your flesh and introduce poisons rendering you paralyzed, but alive none-the-less. Then, they will work their way into your vitals and lay thousands upon thousands of eggs that shall shortly hatch and devour you from the inside out. Do you feel them?"

The cluster of webbing rustled.

"Yes!" came a panicked voice from the webbing. "I feel them! Please, release me! Please!!"

"I've a few questions, then you shall be released. First, where did the pair of you come from?"

"W-we're K-Listers. Washouts looking to man ship. We were in a K-Lister bar on Onaris and we signed on here. The Captain bought the lot. He promised us riches."

"I see, and who bewitched the surviving crew?"

The two crewmen screamed and thrashed in the webbing. "Ah, ah! Get them off! Get them off! Please!!"

"Shall I offer you mercy?"

"Please!!"

"Ah now, your salvation is at hand, never fear. I have an agent that will kill the insects, but first, my previous question stands. Who did this to the crew?"

"Th-the people in the hold. Hold 4!"

"Who are these people in Hold 4?"

"We d-don't know. Strange people, people in robes!! Came with the Xaphan. We stay away from them!"

The two began a fitful round of screaming!

"All right! All right! Enough of your caterwauling. I've administered the agent. The insects are all dead. Do you understand? They are dead and you are in no further danger. Do you feel them dropping off and withering to nothing?"

The crew quieted down and sobbed, thanking their makers, lost in their pliable hallucinogenic dream.

Stenibelle needed them. She could use a gun hand or two should things turn bad when she was ready to fetch Melazarr of Caroline. It was time to turn them to her side. She spoke in a kind voice, a soothing voice. "There now, I have done as you asked and you are safe. Will you admit that I helped you?"

"Yes, yes," one of them said, rather breathless.

"And will you admit that I am kind."

"Yes, you're an angel."

"Neither one of you have any particular allegiance to the Captain or his First Officer, do you?"

"No," the man said.

"No, no," the woman replied.

"And you mentioned money. How much was the Captain offering you?"

"100,000 solaris."

"If I offer to double that sum, will you assist me? I need help and I will pay for your loyalty."

The two struggled with the thought, "We, we . . . the Captain will kill us. The First Officer isn't human. I've seen what she really is."

Not human? That was an odd revelation. Stenibelle needed more information, but she had to be careful, if she got them thinking about the First Officer she would lose her hold on them. She had to divert the conversation.

"Do not worry about the Captain or his First. Understand? Worry about me and what terrible things I can do to you. Perhaps I'm not human either. Care for another go with your insect friends? Perhaps I am an insect. Perhaps I am the Queen of insects."

"No! No, please . . ."

"Are you certain? My children are quite hungry. I have their welfare to think of."

"Yes! No more insects!"

"Then, I may count on your help?"

The two struggled for a moment, "Yes, yes I'll help. I've never liked the Captain much anyway."

"And I'll offer my services! I swear it!" the woman said.

Stenibelle certainly knew that under normal circumstances she couldn't trust these two, they were obviously greedy and unprincipled, but, with the effects of her sting, they should be forced into a more pliable state for an hour or two. With luck, that should be enough.

Stenibelle reached into her HRN and pulled out an inverse green Holystone. She broke it open and the webbing dissolved into a cloying mist. Free, the two crewmen stood up and looked around.

"Ah, that's better," Stenibelle said. "Now, I'll take your weapons for the time being."

They handed over their heat guns. Stenibelle pulled their power packs. She tossed them aside. Lying on the floor at their feet, Lessa struggled and made a series of pained sounds. Stenibelle inspected her; she was burning up with fever. She parted her terrycloth robe and fanned her.

"You two, get her back to the bed!"

They picked her up and trundled her to the bed. They set her down and backed away.

Stenibelle pointed at the woman. "You! What is your name?"

"Julia of Fountain-Locke. I'm from Tubruk."

"Never heard of it. Never been there. Fetch a few wet towels, now!" As commanded, Julia went into the bathroom.

Stenibelle turned to the male crewman. "And you, what is your name?"

"Willard of Falconer. I was a navigator on the *Bellfountain* before I got washed out to the K-List. All I bloody well did was take a bad vector into the Kills and I'm off my chair and on the list." He looked Stenibelle over. "You're really pretty."

It was important to lead the thoughts of a person under the influence of her narcotics, otherwise, if left to themselves, they might snap out of it. "Am I? Well then, perhaps we will fall in love later. For now, what can you tell me about this arcane tattoo on Crewman Lessa's arm? There must be some way to counter it."

"You mean we might screw?" he asked, excited.

"If you please me. And, how do you please me? The tattoo, tell me about it."

"I'm not certain. It has something to do with cultivating Shadow tech from within their bodies. Women only. I recall the Xaphan saying something about cutting across the tattoo and the Shadow tech will drain out."

Crewman Julia returned from the bathroom with the towels. Stenibelle took them and wetted Lessa's burning forehead. "Thank you. Now, I want you to remove that nose ring and wash the horrid paint from your face."

"Why?"

"It distresses me."

Without saying a word, Julia went back into the bathroom and turned the water on.

Stenibelle inspected the tattoo; it was complex with a series of crosshatched lines and dots. Cutting it was worth a try. She produced a MARZABLE dagger. Carefully, she cut Lessa's arm along the length of the tattoo, gently scoring the skin, going a little deeper with every pass. Soon, a torrent of black Shadow tech, like spilling oil, oozed from the cuts. It collected on the bedsheets in an ominous dark mass. Stenibelle was amazed how much came out.

"Once they're ready, they get taken to the hold and they squeeze them. There isn't much left of their bodies afterwards," Willard said.

A Com in Willard's pocket beeped. He was alarmed. "That's the first officer, no doubt, demanding an update."

Stenibelle put her hand to her face—things were happening too quickly, and these two, mucked up by the narcotics, couldn't be counted on for much creative thought on their own. She thought fast. "Tell her I've escaped, but that you have me cornered in the estuary down the aft end of the ship and you will soon have me in custody. If she asks, tell them I am a street urchin stowed aboard from your last port of call."

"Aye." Willard got his Com out and spoke into it.

Julia emerged from the bathroom, her face damp and slightly pink from scrubbing, free of paint, her nose ring gone.

"Much better," Stenibelle said. "Aren't you a sight."

The flow of Shadow tech from Lessa's arm abated and she immediately showed improvement. Her temperature dropped and her heart rate slowed to a more normal pace. "Watch her," she asked Julia and she moved in with a towel.

Stenibelle went to the door and peeked into the hallway. It was empty.

"Willard, I heard tell of the Captain's plan to accost a transport ship and take a number of women. When is that to happen?"

"Soon," he said. "I'm not certain of the time, but we are already en route."

This was too much. Stenibelle had to worry about the welfare of the crew, the lives aboard a transport ship, Melazarr of Caroline and her own skin to boot. She wracked her brains for a plan.

"All right, let's get a Com out. I'm informing the Fleet of the doings on this ship immediately."

Willard shook his head. "Can't, the First has locked out the Coms down here."

"We'll see about that." Stenibelle got the Uni-Mind out and placed it near the Com. It interfaced, grappling with its tiny legs. After a few minutes it indicated NO LINE in holographics and then shut itself down. Stenibelle returned it to her HRN.

"Willard, Julia, which of your quarters is closest?"

"Up on Deck Three." Julia said, "It's not a pretty sight, that's where they've got us all."

Stenibelle checked Lessa over one last time. The Shadow tech appeared to be evacuated from her arm. "Good. Let's go there now. You two wait out in the hallway for me, please. Don't move once you get there. I'll be along in a moment."

They put their towels down and went outside. Alone with Lessa, Stenibelle went to her side. She appeared to be on the verge of waking.

"Lessa, Lessa, can you hear me?"

She coughed and opened her eyes to cloudy slits. She wheezed in a panic. Stenibelle attempted to calm her.

"Shhhh, shhh, you're all right. You're safe now."

"Who are you?"

"I'm a friend. I'm here to help you."

She tried to sit up but Stenibelle held her down. She began to weep.

"Gordon? Where's Gordon?" she sobbed.

"Who's Gordon? Is he, perhaps, that handsome gentleman in your photos?"

"He's my fiancée. Dead . . . oh, I, I think he's dead . . . dead." Lessa became hysterical. "Why did the Captain do this to us?"

Stenibelle tried to console her. "I will find Gordon for you, I promise." She placed a Brown Holystone in her hand and closed her fingers around it.

"I'm going to send you to a safe place now. Things might seem confused for bit. I want you to be strong and gather your wits. In a moment you will find yourself in a large, darkened space. When your eyes adjust to the lighting, you'll see a corridor and then some stairs leading down to a crowded street. All right? You will be on Hoffman Plate, Planet Fall—I know it sounds odd, but that's where you will be. I want you to go directly to the nearest Magistrate's office, I think there's one a short walk from the docks. Ask to speak to Captain Gwendolyn of the Fleet scouting ship *Demophalon John*. Tell Captain Gwendolyn where you are and what has happened on this ship, and then I want you to see a Hospitaler and have yourself checked out. All right? And I promise I will send your Gordon there as well when I find him. Do you understand?"

Lessa nodded.

"Do this for Gordon. Now, ready yourself."

Stenibelle squeezed her fingers into a fist, cracking the Brown Holystone in her palm. A moment later, a gaunt, robed Black Maiden appeared from the shadows, hovering over Lessa's bedside. She screamed as the Maiden knelt down and kissed her on the cheek. The both of them then vanished in a crash of smoke, Lessa now safely across the League on Planet Fall and the Maiden returned to her airy home.

Stenibelle checked her HRN: she only had two Brown Holystones left. One for her and one for Melazarr. Those were her salvation.

She went out into the hallway where Julia and Willard were waiting.

"What the frag happened in there?" Julia asked.

"Nothing. Now, to your quarters. Lead the way," Stenibelle said. They went down the corridor and entered a Lift. Stenibelle faded into the Shadows as the doors opened. Noise and smells of stale liquor and burning menthols blared in and assailed her nostrils. The deck was like a back alley in some seedy town. Garbage lay about in piles, graffiti was painted onto the walls and random K-Lister crewman rolled about, all either drunk, balled-out, kooked up or otherwise medicated into stupors. A crewman staggered up to a convenient wall and urinated. As they passed, the common rooms were set up with tables full of liquors, spirits, menthols of various makes, Remax, Magga tabs, and other recreational drugs. Stenibelle was appalled—even prison at Hagthorpe wasn't this chaotic.

Stepping over trash and kooked-up bodies lying in the walkway, they arrived at Julia's quarters and entered. The interior of her quarters were scrawled with angry, chaos messages.

"Did you do all this?" Stenibelle asked.

"I did."

"Got some untreated anger issues, do you, Julia?"

"I just felt like it."

"I see. What in the Name of Creation is the Captain doing?" she asked.

"He gives us what we want," Willard asked. "Have you ever been on the K-List? Our prospects are zero. We're all angry, We're all rock-bottom here."

Stenibelle fumed. "I've been much worse than on the K-List. I was hauled off my ship in irons. I was Paneled, I paid for my own bloody trial with money my House didn't have. I was put on the bag and made a source of A-List frivolity for months, and then I was sent to prison. Hanging out at some K-Lister bar on Onaris drinking cheap spirits and eating unhealthy bar food sounds like a much more fun proposition. At least through all of that, I kept my dignity intact." She glared at them. "Are either of you carrying drugs?"

Willard and Julia glanced at each other.

"Empty your pockets. Empty your pockets immediately!" Stenibelle ordered.

As commanded Julia and Willard complied. Each pulled out a handful of Magga tabs. Willard also had a fresh pack of Wolf menthols. They both dropped their stashes and let them fall to the floor. "May I have my menthols at least, please?" Willard asked.

"No."

Julia was frustrated. "You're not my mother."

Gods, but did this girl remind her of her obstinate sister Embeth. "And thank Creation for that, for your mother did a poor job raising you. I am much worse than your mother. Remember my insects."

A moment of defiance crossed Julia's brow, but then retreated as she recalled the host of insects coming to devour her.

"So what are we doing?" she asked. "What is our plan?"

Stenibelle went to her Com terminal. "We're going to inform the Fleet of what is happening here. That's what we're going to do."

"A call out will register on the Com's panel up on the bridge."

"I'm certain whoever's manning the Com is balled out or kooked up or enjoying a pack of menthols at the moment. We must risk it."

"But . . ."

"I insist." She gave them both a critical eye. "By the way, turn around, the pair of you."

"Why?"

"Just do it."

Willard and Julia turned around.

FHATOOM!

FHATOOM!

Stenibelle gave them both a fresh stab with her VUNKULA. She gave it to them good, in the butt. And they both stumbled about holding their rears as the effects of the powder and salve took hold in their bloodstreams.

She dashed aside the detritus of empty cups and crumpled wrappers. With a wave of her hand, Stenibelle produced the Uni-Mind and it tapped into the Com terminal. Stenibelle and the two crewman watched as the Uni-Mind interfaced, scrolling through the screens, trying to find a way out of the ship.

"Captain's got everything locked down. Can't get a line out."

The Uni-Mind switched from one source to another, trying to locate an un-secured line. At last, it discovered one and connected.

Stenibelle staggered and clutched her head. More Ceril-Cone information barged in; she had a valid code for every ship in the Fleet, all of them complicated and scrambled. She input the code she wanted and the call went out.

The cone went up. There was Lt. Gwendolyn sitting in her small office. Gwen gazed at her for a long moment.

I see you . . . came into her head.

"Lady Belmont," she said. "This is unexpected surprise." Stenibelle detected a slight smile. She was wearing her cracked watch. "What can I do for you?"

"Gwen," she said. "I'm sorry, may I call you Gwen?"

"Of course. May I call you 'Bel'? That is what you prefer?"

"Yes, you may."

"I . . . was looking at that photo you gave me. I was certain it was a novelty, a fake. I looked at it, down to the pixel, down to the base paper, and it looks completely real. I have a number of questions I would like to ask. Perhaps we could . . ."

"Certainly, but another time. Please listen to me, you must advise the Fleet that the Sprint ship *George Parr* under the command of Captain Duval and his first officer, Lt. Remm Deckard, has been compromised."

"Compromised?"

"The Captain and his First have murdered the crew, others he has placed into stasis."

"A Sprint ship requires a minimum of fifty people to be seaworthy. The Captain and his First could not sail by themselves."

"The Captain has brought on a disposable crew of balled out, kooked up K-Listers from Onaris."

"K-Listers? And why has the Captain done this?"

"The Captain and his First Officer are in party with a Xaphan Warlord named Rodrigo of Burgon and are en route as we speak to attack a helpless transport. This ship must be considered an enemy vessel."

"That is a very serious charge, Bel," Gwendolyn turned to her terminal and checked a few screens. "The *George Parr* is currently under sail for the Hedgepeth."

"No, no, I heard him speak on that. He filed a false flight plan for the Hedgepeth. His real goal is to attack a civilian transport vessel in the Gillman Slot and kidnap the passengers."

"For what purpose?"

"To harvest Shadow tech from their bodies. I don't know what they are planning on doing with it. The Captain is insane."

"For Creation's sake, Captain Duval is a church-going man."

"He is also an anarchist and a Nillist of Punt."

Gwendolyn checked her terminals. "I have no idea what that means. I show no transport traffic in the Gillman slot."

"It's an unregistered Xaphan ship bearing refugees. I can prove what I have just told you. I have just sent a crewman to safety on Planet Fall . . ."

"Planet Fall?"

"Yes, I can do those things. Her name is Lady Lessa of Walpole, a junior assistant in the AV department, and she was held under the influence of a Shadow tech-based sorcery. Many of the surviving crew are in a similar situation and are in need of immediate aid. I have asked her to contact you. She will have much to tell."

"All right, I will await her Com. What about the Engineer? The Boatswain?"

"I don't know about them. I don't know their condition. I assume they are dead."

"Do you know your current position?"

"No."

"What is your situation? Are you safe?"

"Relatively so."

"Do not jeopardize yourself. Contact me again, if possible, at 22 Bells. Are you secure for now?"

"I think so, yes."

"Then keep yourself safe until 22 Bells."

She screened off.

10—THE STATUE MOVED

"Tell me about Rodrigo of Burgon," Stenibelle demanded.

"We don't know much about him. He stays on Deck 2 with the Captain most of the time. Sometimes he goes into the Hold."

"And the tall woman? His Tropist? What of her?"

"She's just always there with him. Never says anything. Just doing that touching thing she does."

Stenibelle thought for a moment. She had to get at Melazarr. She had two brown Holystones left, one for Melazarr and one for her. "Come, we are to Deck 2, and there we shall claim Melazarr of Caroline."

Both Julia and Willard were alarmed. "We can't go up there right now. They are on alert to your presence and have V-Trax'ed the deck. We haven't been administered the antidote. We go up there, we're going to be dead."

Stenibelle grit her teeth. Damn!! She thought some more and changed her tactic.

"I saw a photo in Lady Lessa's camera depicting a group of sinister robed people boarding the ship several months back. Who are they?" Stenibelle demanded. Outside the door was a din of talking and people blundering about. There were shouts and groans, bottles breaking and the lurid sounds of drug-fueled sex.

"They're the Xaphan's servants," Julia said. "They are guarding some sort of treasure in the hold. We were afraid of them and stayed out of their way."

"Down in the holds. That's where they take the women," Willard said. "We aren't permitted to go down there except to take the crew there. They do not come back."

Stenibelle rubbed her chin and thought out loud. "If I can no longer get to them on Deck 2, then I'll need to bring them to me. But where? Burgon kept talking about the hold," She turned to Julia. "In what hold are the Xaphan's servants set up?"

"Hold 4."

"I want to see what's there. Let's go. Lead the way. You two won't see me while we're walking, but I'll be there certain enough."

"But we don't want to see them!" Willard protested.

"I shall protect you. Come now, let's go."

They exited to the noisy, trash-filled hallway and headed for the lift, Stenibelle following from the shadows. She carefully observed the two crewmen, looking for signs of recovery. So far, they both appeared to be under her sway.

They entered the lift and went down to the bowels of the ship to the hold decks. While en route, the Com clicked on.

"What are you two idiots doing?" came the angry voice of Lt. Remm Deckard.

Julia and Willard glanced at each other, then Julia answered. "Ma'am, we are currently searching for the suspected intruder."

"What is taking so long? The Com noted unauthorized activity in crew billet #47S. What did you discover there?"

"Nothing, ma'am. The intruder fled before we arrived."

"And you scanned for use of Gifts?"

"Yes, ma'am. We found nothing."

There was an irritated pause, then: "You are currently in Lift #5. Where are you headed and why?"

Julia appeared stumped and unable to answer. "Ma'am, this is Crewman Willard," he said jumping in. "We are headed to the Ripcar bays to determine if the intruder is attempting to get off the ship."

"We are heading down," Deckard replied. "We shall handle this matter personally. Check the bays and then return to your duty stations. The both of you shall be fortunate if I do not put you off the ship myself." The Com snapped off. Both Julia and Willard appeared quite frightened.

"She'll do it, too," Julia mumbled. "I didn't sign up for this, I just wanted out of Inarri." Her long face mis-matched with her festive pink hair. She reached into her pocket hoping to pop a Magga tab, but her pockets were empty.

Stenibelle was torn between pity for the two and disdain, as they were both addicts and were complicit in the endangerment of the bulk of the crew. "All right, I want you both to do as commanded and then return to your duty stations. And, I am warning you, if you betray me, I shall find you and allow my lovely insects to have another go at your brains, making a spacing seem like a nice cool plunge, understood?"

Willard stood, trying to sort things out in his head. "What insects? Where are they?" he asked. He was recovering from the effects of the narcotics, trying to get his thoughts right.

"They're here," Stenibelle replied cupping her hands and holding them out. Willard dubiously looked at her empty hands. "See them? Glistening, hungry, so soft yet so relentless, ready to feast on your innards one little bite at a time."

Willard stared at her cupped hands. A bead of nervous sweat rolled down his cheek.

Stenibelle kept up the pressure. "Here, want a closer look?" She thrust her hands up into his face and he recoiled. He was still seeing a handful of squirming horrors in Stenibelle's hands.

"No, no . . . please. I'm sorry. I'll do what you say. I swear!"

"Good, very good . . ."

They stood in wretched silence for the remainder of the trip in the lift. It stopped on Deck 5 and the two got out. "One more deck," Julia said as she exited and the doors closed.

Alone in the lift, Stenibelle checked her gear. She shook her hand and two brown Holystones appeared. She was certain the two crewmen would betray her shortly and the ship would be turned out in force against her, but, as long as she held these two stones, she could exit at her whim. She was in no danger and she had to get Burgon and Melazarr of Caroline out of V-Trax poisoned Deck 2 and down in the hold where they would be out in the open. She figured she could go into the hold and interdict Burgon's servants, create chaos, spill his Shadow tech upon the floor, that should bring him running, and, with luck, he'll bring Melazarr with him. Then, she'll crack her on the forehead with the brown Holystone and that will be that.

The lift came to a stop and the doors opened, revealing a lonely workmanlike lower deck thrumming with the sounds of the living ship. Nobody seemed to be present. She walked out, still safely faded into the Shadows. Her various danger detectors immediately went off, vibrating with force deep in the pockets of her HRN. She drew her Grenville 40 just to be on the safe side.

She maneuvered through the twists and turns of the deck and arrived at Hold 4. Three K-Lister crewmen stood in sloppy guard with heat weapons hanging at their sides. The massive outer doors to the hold were closed. She needed an opportunity to enter undetected. The guards certainly weren't overly diligent. They passed the time talking and playing at games of chance. They passed a flask back and forth. One popped a Magga tab and drifted away in kooked-up bliss.

Stenibelle took note of the door lock to the hold. No palm lock this time. Instead, it was a complex, five character glyph. She struggled as more Ceril-Cone information from Professor Shurlamp rattled her brain and once again provided the answers. She knew the code and the guards seemed too kooked up to care. Faded into the Shadows, she walked past the guards, entered the code and the doors to the hold swung open.

She entered and the doors closed behind her.

The lighting within was down and the atmosphere was dank. The metal floor of the hold was covered in a thick layer of loamy earth which smelled heavily of peat. It would have been a rather nice, rich smell had it not been so smothering in the air. The dirt was soft under her boots, like it had been freshly plowed and it was quite thick in the center of the hold, at least several feet deep. Stenibelle had to climb a small mound of it to reach a plateau in the center.

In the center of the hold was a great black statue at least fifteen feet tall. It was seated in a basin or cistern partially filled with thick black fluid.

Shadow tech.

Surrounding the statue was a host of odd, fern-like plants waving in an unfelt breeze. The plants were a dull ochre color, roughly five feet high with a thin, cattail-like stalk supporting a palm-shaped flowering body with five distinct petals or runs pointed upward in a gentle curve. The stalks were situated two-by-two and arranged in messy rows around the perimeter of the cistern. Stenibelle squinted. As she approached, those nearest to her reacted, as if sensing her proximity. They bobbed, their petals flicked and undulated in and out, like a hand opening and closing.

She stepped back. Stenibelle puzzled at the statue. It seemed to be a depiction of a robed female wearing a conical helmet that completely covered her face, revealing no trace of features whatsoever. Was this Burgon's Shadow tech Goddess? And, was this statue supposed to give him the coordinates to Cammara? The man must truly be mad.

Activity farther back in the hold caught Stenibelle's attention. Constructed at the rear of the hold was a large platform surrounded on three sides by great tankards made of a shiny silvery metal. Mounted on top of the platform was a small chamber with a sturdy piston situated over top of it. Piled up near the platform were a number of containers similar to the one Lady Lessa had been confined in. Attending at the platform were several stunted, dwarflike people dressed in coarse robes. Those must be Burgon's servants, Julia had said they were dwarves. In steady, workman-like fashion they hauled the containers to the top of the platform. Opening the containers, they pulled females out who were so bloated they barely looked like people at all, but rather blackened bags of ruddy liquid-filled flesh. The dwarves inspected them and then placed them within the vault-like chamber and sealed it tight. The piston came down and Stenibelle heard the pitiful sound of bones breaking and flesh tearing within the chamber. Thick, black liquid gushed from a spout and drained into one of the tankards.

Stenibelle had witnessed the woman within the chamber being pressed like a grape to harvest Shadow tech. This was the fate that had been awaiting Crewman Lessa and the rest. She was horrified.

Moving up and down the wall was a line of dwarves crawling up the sheer face to the ceiling, moving in antlike procession. They were busy hauling the containers from a service hatch in the ceiling, collecting fresh containers and removing the empties.

Her plan had been to come into the hold and create chaos, she hadn't expected any of this. What should she do? She counted at least twenty dwarves milling about—Punts, Burgon had called them. By the manner in which they lugged the containers, they seemed quite strong and they could cling to the wall. Their full capabilities were unknown. She had no Ceril cone information on them to draw from.

She wished for a moment she had her bolabungs again. She had no idea what to do.

The doors to the hold opened. She heard ragged screams. "Please! I told you everything! I swear it! It was an enchantress who could turn invisible! She tortured us! She made us help her!"

It was Julia, pink haired and face washed, and she was being manhandled by Remm Deckard, dragging her in be the scruff of her neck. Julia gagged and feebly kicked.

"Consider this your punishment for failure. If you're still alive at the end of the hour, we'll let this matter pass."

With one arm, Deckard threw Julia deep into the depths of the hold and the doors slid shut.

All activity stopped. The Punts all turned to Julia as she crawled in the dirt. She tried to cower in the dark, her blinking neon 4D tattoo gave her position away. Several came at her, covering the ground fast and hauled her off her feet to the platform. They stripped her bare and tossed her clothes aside revealing her tattooed and pierced body, all the while she sobbed and begged for mercy. She found none. The dwarves ripped the piercings from her body and she screamed in pain. An empty container was brought up. Two dwarves held her down while a third scratched a black tattoo into her arm, covering one that was already there that said:

JULIA LOVES ????

Julia squirmed in terrified misery. "No! Nooooooo! Go away! Pleease, gohhh away!" she cried. Then: "M-mother! Help me, p-please!"

Stenibelle's conscience was proving to be persistent and inconvenient. She had already used one of her brown Holystones on Lady Lessa, and now here was Julia, a pink haired vagabond from Tubruk, in deep distress. Lessa had deserved to be saved, but Julia? She didn't know this woman, was angered by her sloth. She was complicit in the doings on this ship, and she was going to burn Lessa without hardly a thought. Yet, she couldn't take the sounds of her screams, and if she allowed Julia to suffer this terrible fate, it would be something she would never forget.

She acted. She pulled the hammer on her Grenville 40 and shook her free hand producing three MARZABLE daggers between her fingers. She uncoiled her VUNKULA and readied it for battle. She fired and slashed in with her daggers and engaged the Punt carving the tattoo in Julia's arm. She buried two bullets into his head. The other two spun about, unable to see her. She attacked, the VUNKULA emerging from her HRN like a sledgehammer, blowing the Punts back off the platform. A Punt reached in her direction and she sliced through his arm like soft gelatin. Tepid brackish fluid came gushing out as the Punt uttered a fearful, graveyard cry. She blew his head off with another slug from her gun.

The final Punt, unable to see her, did something completely unexpected. It reached up and ripped its own head off, throwing it to the platform. It reeked of Shadow tech. The head, though disembodied, still lived and it shifted about with snake-like movements. It seemed to see her, though she was faded into the Shadows and uttered a hideous bellow, giving away her position.

More Punts came in, scurrying down the walls, moving with surprising speed. Fresh quarry awaited. They attacked en mass, testing the air, searching for her. The head bounded toward her and latched onto her HRN with its teeth. She kicked it away, shot at it, waved up some red Holystones, and set it on fire.

The Punts came in fast, reaching, grabbing, finding her invisible body. Stenibelle moved to her right and lopped off the limbs of several more Punts, which did not seem to inconvenience them in the slightest. She emptied her Grenville 40 and tossed it aside. She switched back to the VUNKULA and let them have it, rocking them off the platform with devastating blows. Several moved on Julia, and her tortured wails filled the hold.

Stenibelle produced one of her all-important brown Holystones and tossed it at her. It hit her in the back and broke open, the maiden appeared and they were both gone in a smoky flash.

That's it, Julia was now on Planet Fall, she had just saved her. Now, Stenibelle was down to one. Her plan of escaping to Planet Fall with Melazarr was gone. As she fought for her life, Stenibelle vaguely wondered what Julia would do if she ever saw her again. Would she be grateful? Would she offer her thanks, perhaps buy her a beer. Would she have cleaned herself up? Perhaps she'd do none of those things. Perhaps she'd just keep walking down the street.

The Punts were overrunning the platform. She bounded down and sprinted through the soft earth, the Punts hot on her heels following her bootprints in the soft earth. As she neared the statue, the plants surrounding it rustled. Slowly, the earth moved and dark Punt shapes emerged, as if sitting up from being in a reclined position. The "ferns" were actually their forearms and hands extending through the dirt and stretched to an impossible length. They made a droning, chattering sort of sound and they stank of Shadow tech.

She jumped up onto the rim of the cistern and fought them. Her daggers tore through their ranks, dropping bits of flesh and boneless appendages. They backed away as Stenibelle pressed the attack. She drew red Holystones and let them fly. More smoke, more fire. The Punts went up like dried cordwood, burning fiercely but, unfortunately, they didn't fall. They seemed to have an outer husk of flesh that burned readily, revealing a black, utterly alien form within, stunted and bone-like, their bodies hosting a series of curved tubes and protrusions and a compaction of fossilized organs within their ribs. Their heads grew between their shoulders, glaring black eyes stared at her. The fire didn't seem to harm them in the least, instead it liberated them. It was like fighting demons.

The Punts regrouped and counter-attacked, pressing forward in a relentless wave. They pulled the heads off of their own bodies, revealing a ruggose orange-skinned, green-haired face under the robes. They then lobbed the heads in her general direction like dire grenades. They hit the floor of the hold and bounced like a rubber ball, Shadow tech spewing from their mouths in a spray like hot tar. Shadow tech rained down on her, she could feel its effects, the frigid tears, the toxic caress, draining the life from her. The onslaught was devastating and Stenibelle had to back away.

Clenched hands came forward searching for her invisible body. One found her leg and locked on. Another had her, and then another. She hacked and slashed but it did little good. Dozens of hands had her. She fell out of the Shadows and Punts reached for her throat. They locked on and pierced her flesh with their horrid claws. Shadow tech was pumped in and she felt it coursing into her system, poisoning her. She felt herself drifting into unconsciousness. She had a number of reagents and poison neutralizers in the deep pockets of her HRN, but she had nothing to counteract Shadow tech.

Use your last Holystone!

I can't! I don't have the data!

Her vision went fuzzy. In desperation, she launched her VUNKULA. She felt the battle club clamp on to the statue behind her and she grappled up the side, finding a nook to crawl into. The Punts assaulted her with a steady stream of heads, arms, legs and other body parts lobbed up from below.

She felt a great shudder, as if the ground beneath her were shaking. The Punts below stopped what they were doing and backed away. Struggling to remain conscious, she vaguely puzzled at what was happening. She heard metal bending and joints creaking. A great hand came up and plucked Stenibelle from her position.

You can't stay here! You've got to go!

She waved up her final brown Holystone to flee, to get away, her mission a failure. Perhaps she was hallucinating, so much Shadow tech in her system, but the statue of the Shadow tech Goddess was *moving* with steady, fluid life. She was placed in the statue's palm. A gigantic helmeted head stared down at her.

Stenibelle tried to crack the Holystone open in her fist, but was too weak. It fell from her hand to the floor far below, lost.

She closed her eyes and awaited her death. She wondered about her House, her father, her sisters, her passed away mother, and how she'd failed them all.

11—CAPTURED

Her mind was in a chaos place on the verge of delirium. She saw herself as a different person, a tall person, standing on a wind-whipped cliff overlooking a vast valley overgrown with virgin trees and patches of ancient grass as far as the eye could see.

A slender pair of arms came around her, holding her tight. A platinum watch sat on the right wrist.

Come on, Bel, let's find some shelter.

Gwen??

Something touched her and she was returned into her body.

When Stenibelle opened her eyes she was no longer in the hold. Gone were the dim lighting and the smothering blanket of earth. Gone were the Punts and the giant statue. Instead, bright lights coming down from above blinded her and the delicate fragrance of tea simmering tickled her nose. Quiet music played. Something fibrous and pine-scented was stuck in her mouth. She reached up to try to remove the foreign object from her mouth, but failed. She couldn't move her arms. She was shackled to a wooden chair with thick manacles, the attached chains trailed down around the back of the chair wrapping around her boots. Her HRN was gone. Her VUNKULA was gone along with the rest of her weapons. The Uni-Mind? Where was it? To her left was a row of windows, cheery and sea-like filled with a glittering curtain of stars. To her right was a paneled wall. A black arcane box the size of a large birdcage sat quietly near the windows. It was Rodrigo of Burgon's mysterious Trempalar Box.

She appeared to be captive in the luxurious upper levels of the ship somewhere; the poison V-Trax gas gone. Bolted to the wall was some sort of hermetic pressure capsule with a hatch large enough for a person to enter. It was hulking and brutish in design, painted a heavy-duty white and deeply scratched from use. It didn't look like something belonging on a Fleet ship. Nearby, a large wardrobe on wheels sat innocently by the windows. It bore the initials RB in hammered lettering, no doubt for Rodrigo of Burgon.

She felt terribly sick and her entire body hurt. Whatever was stuffed into her mouth she gagged on it.

A pair of soft hands came to her face. There was Melazarr of Caroline before her on her knees, her yellowy lion's eyes fixed and clouded with drugs. Her expression was blank, slightly confused. Stenibelle tried to speak, but the wooden device in her mouth prevented her from saying anything. Melazarr gently caressed her cheek and lightly touched her ears. Melazarr's touch was electric and distracting, rather like Morgan's cold touch that had driven her insane with bliss, only Melazarr's was gentle and warm. Stenibelle tested her shackles and they were solid. She waved up a lock pick and maneuvered it into position to get at the lock. The lock was behind her back. She couldn't see what type of lock it was, she would simply have to use what she had and hope for the best. Though shackled, she wondered at her good fortune. Here was Melazarr, the very woman she needed to complete her mission, now if only she could get free and take Melazarr before anybody else arrived. She searched for the lock, nimbly testing the chain with her pick.

Too late. A nearby door opened and through it came the First Officer, Lt. Remm Deckard.

Remm Deckard, *extremely dangerous* came the Ceril.

"What are you doing?" she said in an angry voice as she surveyed the situation. "Get away!" She thundered up and kicked Melazarr to the floor. She groaned in vague pain. Deckard put her oversized Fleet boot on her neck and pressed down hard. Melazarr choked and turned blue. She slowly kicked and thrashed about.

Stenibelle worked furiously, searching for the mechanism. She had to free herself and help Melazarr.

Remm Deckard noticed Stenibelle struggling. "Oh, awake are you?" She hauled back and kicked her in the chest, knocking her over. Stenibelle wheezed, almost dropping her lock pick. She held on tight. Deckard reached down and seized Stenibelle by the neck. Stenibelle felt the hand at her throat get hot, blazing hot, excruciating as if her hand were made of molten lead. Her skin was burning.

Screaming like a child, Melazarr rose up and beat Remm Deckard in the back, flailing away with her fists. The blows sounded hard. Deckard released Stenibelle and put both hands on Melazarr's face, driving her into the floor. She gibbered in agony. Her headband started smoking, as if ready to catch fire. It fell off her head.

Feeling the slow glow of rage form within her, Stenibelle found the locking mechanism and began working it. Another few moments she should be out, and then she, unarmed, would come to grips with Remm Deckard.

She's not human, Willard had said. She didn't think she had enough to beat Deckard without her weapons, but she had to try, for Melazarr and for her House.

The door opened and Rodrigo of Burgon and Captain Duval entered. Burgon saw what was happening and his eyes flared with anger. "Unhand my Tropist and touch her never again, or I shall open my deadly box and allow you to be consumed!"

Deckard released Melazarr drawing her ugly knife from her coat. "Go ahead, open your box. I want to see what's in there. Go ahead!"

"Lt.," Captain Duval said, nonplussed, "be at ease and show a bit of courtesy to our Xaphan guest."

"His bitch was helping the prisoner escape!"

Burgon offered a greasy smile. "She is no prisoner. This lovely woman is our guest."

"Whatever! Your Tropist was pawing her like a monkey and I didn't like it."

Burgon picked up Melazarr's headband and neatly placed it back on her head. "There, there," he said to her in a gentle voice. "My Tropist is topped off with a cocktail of euphoriants keeping her in a sedate state. She could do no such thing."

Deckard stood fast for a moment and glanced at Burgon's sinister black box, then she put her knife away and stepped back. Burgon assisted Melazarr to a nearby couch where she resumed her uncomfortable, trance-like position. Despite being a Xaphan warlord and a cannibal, he seemed to treat Melazarr with a fair amount of tenderness.

"Now then," he said. "Let us look over our guest." He approached Stenibelle and righted her chair. He gazed at her with his micro-second handsome piggy face. "Ah, awake at last, I see. The Shadow tech my friends were kind enough to pump into your flesh has been neutralized. The wood from the Kentralla tree absorbs Shadow tech nicely." He pulled a wooden bit out of her mouth and examined it. Satisfied, he tossed it aside. "The threat of poisoning is gone. You are safe."

The Captain fetched a cup of tea and seated himself. Remm Deckard stood next to him.

"So, what did you find, anything?" Burgon asked. "Did you find the substance she drugged us with?"

"Found lots of things," Deckard stated flatly. On a table behind Deckard was Stenibelle's kit: her HRN, her VUNKULA and her other assorted accessories. Deckard rummaged through her items. "She was armed with a Grenville 40 pistol that had been recently fired, a very well-made VUNKULA with a Hoban War Club tip, and an old Hoban Royal Navy coat full of a number of novel accessories which I'm still sorting through. Our friend here seems to be a wood-be alchemist."

"I've no doubt, given the chemicals she plied us with earlier. Where did she get a VUNKULA from?" Duval asked. "She's no Grenville, I know all of the Grenvilles. She looks more like an Esther woman to me: small, nice serviceable hips, pretty face. She probably bedded somebody for it. Was it Geyron? It was, wasn't it? He has a weakness for Esther beauties."

Stenibelle didn't answer, but he was correct. Geyron of Grenville had taught her the VUNKULA's use.

Bel, you are the most beautiful woman I have ever known. I'd wear a thousand VUNKULAs if only to embrace you with all of them.

Remm Deckard held up the small shiny form of the Uni-Mind. "She also had this, it's some sort of communications device. What information did you steal with this?"

Stenibelle felt her heart skip a beat. She remained silent.

"Well then, look." Remm Deckard's hand became red hot, the Uni-Mind began glowing.

"Don't destroy it, Lt., it might contain valuable information," Duval said. "We'll hack in and decipher it later." Deckard relented and set it down on the table.

"Who are you working for? How did you get aboard this ship?" Deckard demanded.

Nothing, silence. Remm Deckard became impatient.

"So, why is this person up here and not in a container growing fat in the hold with Shadow tech? You need females, well, here's one. Leave her to her fate, that's the price of being a spy."

Burgon took exception. "Because, ignorant woman from Famora, the statue moved in her presence. That is what we have been working for, laboring for, life from the statue. The statue is a *Merten*, it carries messages from the Universe. We have failed thus far with Shadow tech, yet, this woman succeeded merely with her presence. This woman is our key to Cammara."

Merten? Stenibelle mused. A-Ram and Alesta had also used the term *Merten,* some sort of herald bearing the Universe's news. An Extra-Planar entity. Burgon seemed to have his Extra Planar concepts down, but he had badly misidentified the *Merten*—it wasn't the statue in the hold, it was Melazarr of Caroline sitting right next to him half naked in a trance. Fortunately, the truth evaded him and he seemed confident in his faulty knowledge. That, at least, was working in her favor.

Deckard picked up a report and looked it over. "Really? Her name is Stenibelle, 30th daughter, House of Belmont-South Tyrol. So, you were right, Captain, she is an Esther. She was formerly a Fleet Paymaster serving aboard the Warbird *New Faith.*"

"The House of Tyrol is known on Kana for practicing sorcery," Duval added. "I've read about that."

"Sorcery? That could be significant," Burgon said.

"I don't see how," Deckard said. "This little elf bought the chair of the old Fleet ship *Seeker* before it got smelted down last year, but she didn't last long. She was remanded into custody for violating sea lanes, for assaulting a Fleet Yardmaster and for general incompetence of command. She was paneled, thrown on the bag and then was sentenced to ten years in Hagthorpe Prison. According to our records, she was recently released from prison on a Rights technicality." Deckard put the report down. "Like I said, she doesn't seem like much to me."

"Your thoughts are noted, Lt., however, the statue moved in her presence, we all saw it and there can be no doubt. That is the sign we have been looking for," Burgon said.

"Well then, let's get her back down there and get the statue going. What are we waiting for?"

Burgon would not be rushed. "Have a bit of patience. I want to understand what we are dealing with first." Burgon approached her, sizing her up like a show animal. "Lady Stenibelle? Can you speak?"

Stenibelle stayed quiet.

Remm Deckard thundered forward and wrenched her head back. "He asked you a question, you prison slut Johnnywag—talk!"

Nothing.

Deckard pointed at the scratched-up white capsule bolted to the wall. "You see that? It's a custom addition. We call it 'The Hatch'. That's where we sent out all the male crew members. We couldn't use the airlocks, all of their activity is archived and monitored at Fleet. We can, however, use 'The Hatch' all we want. We just marched them in and put them out like so much garbage. Your friend, what's-his-name, your K-Lister accomplice, tried it out not long ago. Care to follow him?"

Willard of Falconer was dead. Spaced.

He hadn't seemed like such a bad fellow. Maybe all he needed was a sympathetic ear, a pep talk, a kick in the rear and possibly a second chance. She herself had needed those things not long ago and had people who cared enough to give them to her. Now he was gone, his body never to be found. He hadn't deserved that.

She grieved for him, a sob escaping her lips.

"Oh, what's the matter, hon, scared?" Deckard said.

Burgon was annoyed with Deckard's tactics. "Are you certain you're not a Xaphan, Lt.? You seem to have a propensity for hasty decisions and rash violent acts. Very Xaphan-like. We are not putting her out the ship!" he said. "Now please, step back and be seated. I shall attend here."

Deckard smiled. She took a small breath of air and blew into Stenibelle's face. Very quickly the heat of her breath became scorching, became unbearable, like dragon's breath. Stenibelle was being burned by Deckard's breath as if there were a raging furnace within her.

Stenibelle's face red, Deckard snickered and seated herself near the captain.

"I am sorry for that," Burgon said to Stenibelle. "I'll wager there has not been a moment in your life when you thought a Xaphan Warlord would be your greatest advocate and defender. Now then, what know you of the Shadow tech Goddess? Anything? Have you studied her in your sorcerous learnings? Shall I tell you? The Shadow tech Goddess is a fabled spirit, a deity if you will. Her role is to serve as the Universe's protector and sentinel. She determines who lives and who dies. She punishes those seeking to circumvent the Universal scheme. In some places where her services are not required, she is a simple mortal woman living an unremarkable life. In others where she is needed, she is a destroyer sitting on her iron throne in the places between all things. When she emerges from her hidden place, nothing is left but Shadow tech, they say it bleeds from her womb and she is its mother. Shadow tech, despite its apparent destructive power, is the basis of life. Just like a raging fire that leaves a blackened forest ripe for re-growth, what the Shadow tech Goddess destroys is fertile ground for the re-creation of life, just waiting for someone to come and give it proper shape. We in Punt intend to be the progenitors of a new universe, built in our design, shaped to our specifications, where we are the gods. We have been planning for centuries how our universe shall evolve. Oh, it will be glorious, stunning, unimaginable. All we need is to bring the Shadow tech Goddess forth and let her do her work, but, that task has not been easy. She sits, just beyond our reach. We've tried everything. We've sacrificed millions, we've sullied twice-fold. We've sung, we've danced, we've beaten our drums and burned whole civilizations to the ground, and still she will not come. We, however, will not be denied. Our sages recently discovered ancient wisdom regarding our mistress. We discovered we had been coming at this problem wrong-footed, all that killing and burning and debauching was for nothing, our mistress is beyond those things. We discovered the existence of a forgotten shrine in a faraway place. The shrine, according to our research, is a cursed place inhabited by a loathsome demon. But, also within the shrine is a wondrous key known in the learned circles as the Anatameter."

Anatameter.

The name rang through her and struck deep. It was a word she knew, had heard many times, A-Ram and Alesta had mentioned it. She had also heard the name, but not with her ears. Other versions of herself had heard it, had struggled with it, had held it in their hands.

Burgon saw her react. "Yes, the name rings with you, doesn't it? All we need do is go to the shrine and turn the Anatameter's knob, and then there is the Shadow tech Goddess just a short walk away."

Captain Duval shrugged and set his tea cup down. "Yes, but we don't know the way to the shrine, do we, Burgon? With you, everything's a dead end."

Burgon flushed with anger. "If all this was easy, it would have been done long ago, wouldn't it? And, to correct you, sir Captain, we are not at a dead end. It's a four step process. The Statue knows the way to Cammara. The Gods of Cammara know the way to the shrine, we go to the Shrine and turn the knob of the Anatameter and then we go to the Shadow tech Goddess. First thing's first: the Statue must tell us the way to Cammara."

He turned back to Stenibelle. "The great *Merten* statue you gave life to in the hold, we stole it from an old goddess temple in Ming Moorland where she was said to perform miracles given the correct circumstances. She knows the way to the Gods of Cammara." Burgon paused and regarded her, looking for insight.

"So, why her?" Duval asked. "Why is she special? Why did the statue move?"

"Let us find out." Burgon went to his wardrobe and opened it. Inside was a collection of arcane accessories, rare fabrics and stacks of vellum. "Let us find out right now."

Burgon rummaged through his wardrobe and pulled out several items of Xaphan design. He washed them with scented oil poured from a jug. Stenibelle glanced at Melazarr, sitting silent nearby, not having moved a muscle. Her throat was slightly swollen from Deckard's boot.

Melazarr is the Merten, not the bloody statue.

He returned with his freshly oiled implements and inspected Stenibelle with them, running them up and down her body getting oil on her shirt.

"I'm sorry I dirtied your shirt. We shall soon get you out of these clothes and into something more flattering for a lady such as yourself. Hmmmm," he mumbled with interest.

"What have you discovered?" Duval asked.

He performed more tests.

"Burgon?"

He went to his wardrobe and pulled a creaky old book from the lower shelves. He opened it and leafed through the pages. He took his time. He found what he wanted and traced through the text with his finger. He smiled, set the book aside and put his things away. "We are in rare company, Captain," he announced. "Lady Stenibelle is a *Kaidar Gemain*." He stood there, smiling, considering the possibilities. He opened and closed his fist in excitement.

"What's that?" Remm Deckard asked. "'Whore' in Xaphan?"

"Hardly. It means she is an Extra-Planar Entity, exceedingly rare. Extra-Planar Entities are beings who hold a special place in the Universe, they are those who may break the bonds of time and space. In some cases they are the living 'pulse' of the Universe, they enjoy the Universe's favor. In some cases they bear messages from the universe that only the wise and the diligent can read—our statue in the hold is a *Merten*, an Extra-Planar Entity. The *Kaidar Gemain* is the greatest of the lot. She exists in every universe. There is not one where she is not present. That is unheard of."

"So?" Deckard said flatly.

"Yes, Burgon, what does this mean?" Duval asked.

Burgon muttered to himself in an odd tongue. "It means our gateway to the Gods of Cammara is soon to be open. A *Kaidar Gemain* is a creature of immense power. With Lady Stenibelle at our side, portals open, old gateways become active and locked doors in hidden places unlock. She breathes life into that which is lifeless, and the statue lives in her presence. And now, a *Kaidar Gemain* has fallen square into my lap."

"*Our* lap, you mean," Duval said. "So, if I am reading you correctly, our mission is complete? We no longer need to harvest Shadow tech?"

"That is incorrect. The harvesting must continue until we stand on Cammara. We must have a gift to offer the Gods. Casks flowing with Shadow tech shall do nicely, I think." Burgon was fascinated by Stenibelle. He closely examined her face, poked and prodded her and tested her chains. "I wish her released."

Duval didn't react. "She stays where she is," Deckard replied.

"After we've secured our latest offering, I shall allow her to be released, under heavy sedation," Duval said.

"Into my custody, yes?" Burgon said.

"Into our joint custody. She is just as much mine as she is yours, and more so mine, as you stand on my ship, under my guns." Duval stood and approached, giving Stenibelle an invasive glance in his Remnath fashion. "Are you certain this woman is something special? She looks like a standard Esther girl to me. She is pretty, certainly, but there are many pretty girls from Esther. How did you come to this conclusion?"

Burgon went to his wardrobe and fetched an empty picture frame from the clanking curtains of junk within. He returned and held it up in front of Stenibelle. Faces appeared in the frame, a multitude of them, a never-ending parade of them.

"This is her in her infinite guises as *Kaidar Gemain*. And look!" Burgon cried. "In every other universe, she is a man. How remarkable!"

"Does that mean anything?" Duval asked.

"Only that we here are privy to the most lovely aspect of this Extra-Planar Entity. With our Lady Stenibelle here, it shall be we who dictate terms in the court of Mons Eagle on Cammara. The Gods will hear our discourse."

He came in and took her by the chin and whispered. "You shall be my constant consort. With you at my side, nothing is out of bounds. We may have whatever we want. You shall never be far from my side again."

Stenibelle gurgled a little. She was mostly acting, lulling Burgon into thinking she was insensate. She could have her lock picked at any time. She had to be careful and choose her moment to strike carefully.

Burgon fished through his wardrobe and pulled out a small brazier, an onyx jug and a stout metal brand.

Behind Stenibelle, Melazarr stirred a little. She could feel Melazarr's eyes fixed on her.

"Muh, muh , muh . . ." she muttered, breathless.

No, no!! Not now!! She might speak the secret, and then Burgon would realize his mistake and he would have it, and she could not allow that.

"Shut your Tropist up, Burgon!" Remm Deckard said. "Or, I'll put my boot down her throat again."

Melazarr stood on her long legs and tottered about in a daze, heading toward Burgon's wardrobe. As she passed Stenibelle, her fingers brushed past her wrist. Her touch was magnetic, doing all sorts of naughty things within her body, arousing her. She pulled out a roll of vellum and a marker. Burgon approached and gently put his arms around her.

"There, there," he said. He returned her to her pillow and seated her.

Seated, Melazarr began furiously scribbling on the vellum, the marker flying across the page. "Muh, muh. muh . . ." she mumbled over and over.

She was drawing a chart to Cammara, Stenibelle could see it.

"What is she doing?" Duval asked. Burgon was busy setting up his brazier. He glanced at the markings she was making on the vellum but dismissed them as mere scribbles.

"Nothing. Just random drawings. She does them on occasion. The drugs I give her tend to make her rather child-like and insensate. They are meaningless."

Stenibelle could not let them discover the import of Melazarr's drawing.

Just then the Com rang in. "Sir," came a voice from the bridge.

"What is it?" Duval replied.

"We are approaching the Gillman Slot."

"Ah," Duval said, "at last. Have we located our promised catch for the day?"

"Aye, sir, six thousand KV's and closing."

"Bring us in and disable the vessel. Prepare a docking party. Full salvage rights are in effect. Just a moment, we'll be right there." He put his tea cup aside and stood. "Lt., would you please take command on the bridge and supervise the taking of our quarry. I don't trust this K-Lister lot."

"Aye." She turned and exited the door.

"And nor should you, Captain," Burgon said. "Vulgar, the lot of them." He mixed chemicals and a bluish fire jumped about in the brazier pan and sizzled.

Remm Deckard's voice came in from the Com a few minutes later. "Captain, we have a visual on the Xaphan ship. It looks to be an old *Merci* 2. She's seen us and is running."

Captain Duval smirked. "Is she? Oh, what are we to do, I wonder? We certainly can't match sails with a hundred year old Xaphan *Merci* 2, can we? Get them, Lt. These K-Lister lot need their salvage and pint of blood, don't they? Catch that ship and let us feast hearty."

"Aye."

"And then, it is time. We make sail for Xaphan space. I am ready to begin our journey to Cammara."

"We don't have the data just yet," Burgon said.

"But we will, Our little *Kaidar Gemain* will get it for us, yes?"

Duval wandered over to Melazarr and watched her work. She was leaning over, babbling slightly, scratching hard on the vellum.

"I'm curious what she's doing, Burgon. She seems to be working with conviction and intent."

Burgon opened his jug and poured a thick pearly liquid into the fire, followed by his brand, allowing it to get hot. "I told you it was nothing."

"It doesn't look like nothing to me. It looks like she's composing a detailed stellar chart."

"What?"

Stenibelle had to do something to divert their attention. Her sister Elma had a habit of screaming when she wanted attention, uttering a heart-stopping, blood curdling, ear-bursting scream that could be heard from one end of Belmont Manor to the other. Stenibelle opened her mouth and screamed as loud as she could, getting her lungs into it. Both Burgon and Captain Duval were put off.

"Gods, what is wrong with her?" Duval asked.

"Perhaps your thug First Officer injured her." He patted her shoulder. "Be calm, I'll have you out of this chair in no time. Just have to take care of one small thing first."

The fire in his brazier popped. The brand began to glow.

Remm Deckard's voice came back down over the Com. "Sir! We are unable to catch the Xaphan ship!"

Duval turned to the Com in frustration. "Impossible. There is no ship type in the Xaphan armada that a Sprint-class ship such as ours can't outrun, especially an Elder-down *Merci 2*."

"They are doing it, sir! We are at full sub-SM rotations and losing ground."

"Tuck in and catch that ship, Lt.!"

"Aye!"

Melazarr finished drawing. She sat back. "Muh, muh, muh . . . map to cammara . . ." she mumbled.

"What was that, deary?" Duval asked. "Say again."

Stenibelle screamed again, trying to capture his attention.

"MAP TO CAMMARA!" Melazarr screeched. "MAP TO CAMMARA!!"

Duval stepped over to Melazarr. He pulled the vellum roll away from her and looked at it. He sucked in his breath.

"Burgon! This is a very detailed stellar chart. Look, there are meridians, and vectors. I recognize these constellations and other stellar bodies. There are proper declinations and ascensions, there are reference points, tables and conversions to AM/PM." He gasped. "This is a chart to Cammara at long last."

Burgon pulled the metal brand out of the fire. It was sizzling hot. "Is it? How is it she knows the way to Cammara? She knows nothing of such things. She is my Tropist, that is all."

Duval stood there holding the chart. "Perhaps you've miscalculated. It wouldn't be the first time, would it? Perhaps she's one of these Extra-Planar beings you mention. They seem to be coming out the woodwork at the moment." He looked at the flaming brand in Burgon's hand. "What are you doing with that?"

"I'm going to brand Lady Stenibelle with my Chastity Key. She will never be far from my side again, then we can have a look at this silly drawing my Tropist made."

Burgon moved toward Stenibelle, his brand steaming. A Xaphan Cabalist symbol was embossed at the tip. "Now, help me lift her chin a little . . . I'm aiming for the base of her neck."

Stenibelle moved in a flash. She sprung the lock and surged from the chair, surprising Burgon with the speed of her attack. She waved up three MARZABLE daggers and slashed at him. He dropped his brand in shock.

"Com, the prisoner is escaped!" Duval cried backing away. "V-Trax Deck 2 immediately!"

She faded into the Shadows and came at Duval, hoping to snatch the chart away from him. He backed away, holding it tight and drawing his MiMs pistol. "V-Trax the deck now!"

A sweet-smelling pinkish gas snaked in through several vents.

"Where did she go!" Burgon roared.

Faded and invisible, Stenibelle moved fast. She didn't have long until the V-Trax gas incapacitated her.

She grabbed her VUNKULA off the table and quickly strapped it on, cinching the buckle, feeling the metal tail come to life.

POCK! POCK! Duval popped off a few shots in her direction, bad misses.

Burgon came in. "What are you doing? Don't shoot, you might kill her! Lady Stenibelle, stop! I cannot protect you if you try to escape! Be reasonable! Where are you to go?"

She responded by savagely smashing him in the cheek with the VUNKULA, the blow sending him flying to the ground.

His Trempalar Box shuddered with eager movement, waiting to open up. She seized the box with her VUNKULA and stuffed it into The Hatch. She pulled the lever, the hatch closed and the box was flushed out into space, floating past the windows and was gone.

The gas was filling the room. She had to get out. She seized the Uni-Mind and her HRN and took Melazarr by the wrist, jerking her along. Melazarr limply followed, her bare feet slapping on the floor tiles, her eyes vacant. She was like a giant child, barely aware of what was happening around her.

Stenibelle tried the door. Locked, just like before, the Chastity Key branded into Melazarr's flesh was hindering her exit. The thought that she was only seconds away from being branded herself made her shudder.

POCK! POCK! More shots from Duval, putting tiny holes through the door.

The gas was becoming too much. She coughed.

She smashed through the door with several hammer blows from the VUNKULA, the door broke in two. She fled out into the corridor with Melazarr, bewildered and gangly at her side. She barricaded the door with the table as she exited. She knew the lifts would be locked down by now, so she used her Ceril-Cone information. Ahead was J-34, a maintenance tube that headed down two decks. She opened it, threw Melazarr in and crawled in after her. Closing it up, she heard Burgon and Duval surge into the corridor along with a third voice: Remm Deckard's.

"What happened? I knew it!!" she roared. "That little bitch!"

Leading the way, she twisted and turned, through the tight passages, pulling Melazarr along. She smiled slightly, as if playing a game.

Somehow, they managed to escape from Deck 2 and its toxic gas and retreat to the lower decks.

12—Ambush

Hiding in the tube, Stenibelle moved Melazarr along until she thought it safe to pause a moment deep in Deck 6. She took inventory of her things. She had her VUNKULA, which was a blessing, and her MARZABLE daggers which they hadn't detected. She had most of her Holystones and most of her arcane kit which were still in their pockets. She slapped her HRN pockets in a mild panic. There was the Uni-Mind, she was relieved.

Her Grenville 40 was missing. No matter. She rarely used it anyway. Of course, her brown Holystone was gone, lost in the hold in the battle with the Punts.

All the while she was going through her things, Melazarr was restless and rather difficult to handle. Drugged and sluggish, she pawed at her, trying to get at her wrists. Whenever she did manage to touch them, the surge of pleasure her touch created was quite astounding.

Even more astounding was the image that flashed through her mind:
Gwen
Gwen touching her.
She loved her as a man, why not as a woman?
Why not??

They couldn't stay in the tube for long, Duval and Remm Deckard would send armed crawlers after them, though the size of the ship would shelter them temporarily. Her Ceril cone information told her that the safest place to hide on the ship would be the ship's tailoring office on Deck 7, which was not heavily scanned, camera'ed or traveled. Dragging Melazarr along, which was becoming increasingly difficult, they made their way to the tailoring office. Melazarr was grabby and childlike, pulling on her coat, on her boots, pulling items out of her pockets. She seemed to want to play fight and got her into a headlock, and with her size and weight it was wrenchingly tight. One time, she turned and presented herself, as if she wanted to have sex. Stenibelle moved her along as best she could.

There was the tailoring office. Faded, Stenibelle went first. The office was locked and apparently disused. The Chastity Key on Melazarr's neck was proving to be inconvenient and the lock would not budge. Instead, Stenibelle located an air vent and they went in. Inside, she found the tiny office empty. She returned to the tube and dragged Melazarr in, seating her in a corner. She seemed unsettled and rank. Perhaps she missed Burgon's presence. He had demonstrated a fair amount of tenderness toward her. Stenibelle tried to get her to draw another map to Cammara, as she had done earlier, but she was unresponsive and uninterested in anything but wrestling and having sex. Stenibelle gave her a few items from her HRN to play with and that seemed to calm her a little. Outside, she could hear the occasional passing of crew and, once, she thought she smelled the acid perfume of Shadow tech.

She had to know what was happening on the bridge, and she had to figure out a way off the ship. Stenibelle found a Com node and decided to risk connecting the Uni-Mind. She had to have information.

She got the Uni-Mind out and deployed it. Despite Remm Deckard having heated it up to cherry red, it still worked as normal. Masterfully, it hacked into the ship's Com node.

Information flowed in, a cone of sound opened.

Lots of chatter. Many voices. Gruff K-Lister voices, some spoiling for her hide, along with more subdued regulars trying to run the ship. She listened carefully and sorted out the ones she thought most important.

Duval: "They must still be using the tubes. Get crawlers. Deploy in Deck 3 forward and scout aft, deck by deck."

Deckard: "When they are found, shoot to kill."

Duval: "Countermanded. We've covered this ground before, Lt.. Neither is to be killed. The Caroline Tropist is to be returned to Burgon and the Esther is to be stripped of her weapons, branded, drugged and left in my charge. After we capture the Xaphan ship, we shall make sail for Bustoke, provision up and then get under way for Cammara. I am convinced this chart is good. I am eager to put sail to the League."

Com: "Sir! Our target vessel has vanished! It seems to have been a sensor mirage implanted into our main deck."

Sensor mirage? Implanted? Stenibelle wondered if the "mirage" had somehow been the doing of Professor Shurlamp. And if that was the case, then she must have lured the *George Parr* to this area of space. The question was why?

There were a few moments of cold silence, of confusion.

Duval: "Vanished?"

Com: "It's gone, sir. We are, however, detecting a vessel entering the theatre from 7:30PM. It is flying the colors of the 3rd Fleet, scouting division. It is the *Demophalon John.*"

The *Demophalon John.* Gwen! She had come.

Duval: "What is a scouting ship doing out here? You checked the flightways for traffic, yes?"

Com: "Aye, nevertheless, she is here and she is sounding Council. Her Captain wishes to come aboard."

Duval: "Is she flying an Admiral?"

Com: "No sir."

Another short pause.

Duval: "We shall respond to her hails, allow her to come in. We shall then loiter to her rear, and, when in position, we shall open fire and take out her engines and mast. Then, her crew shall be prime for our taking. If we'll not have a Xaphan ship, a League ship will do, and out here nobody will be the wiser. We're soon to quit the League until we return as destroyers."

Gwen! She'll be killed!

Duval: "Please inform me when the ship is in position. Easy now, patience, we're all friends here."

Com: "Aye, sir, she's coming in now."

Stenibelle sucked in her breath and grit her teeth.

It's a trap, Gwen!!

Com: "The scouting ship is in our forward firing envelope."

Duval stayed silent. On came Remm Deckard's voice.

Deckard: "Mark bearings and fire."

The ship shuddered and the weapons uncoiled.

Gwen!!

Deckard: "Damage report!"

Com: "Miss! The scouting ship deployed its maneuvering canards and turned away. The scouting ship just turned us to broadsides and is opening-fire!"

The ship trembled and yawed a bit, Stenibelle could feel it. It was being pounded by weapons fire.

Deckard: "Return fire! Disable that ship!"

Com: "Our targeting scanners have been knocked out!"

Deckard: "For Creation's Sake, then aim manually!"

Com: "Captain, a pair of Marine *Ballista*-class Cutter ships of the 13th Stellar Operations Division have appeared off our baffles!! They are coming in fast. We are going to be boarded!"

Stenibelle was overjoyed. Gwendolyn had come, and she brought the Marines with her.

Another pause. Duval came back on.

Duval: "For the love of Creation! Send to Fleet. Advise we are under attack and under Board by Fleet assets and demand intervention! Swing around and get us out of here, flanking speed!"

The ship was rocked by another devastating hit.

Com: "Captain, the Marines have disabled our aft thermoplant and we can no longer achieve Stellar mach! We are about to be boarded!"

Duval: "Advise Fleet we are under Board and have sustained casualties. We are returning fire. We must appear to be the wounded party here!"

Then, to Lt. Deckard.

Duval: "Lt., get to the hold and incinerate the crew under stasis. I want no trace left. Com, redact these logs! Our voyage to Cammara will have to wait, until then we are simply an innocent ship on patrol attacked, fired upon and boarded without provocation and that's what I shall argue before the Fleet."

Deckard was coming to kill what was left of the crew. Once again her conscience got the better of her. Stenibelle could not allow that. She pulled the Uni-Mind and went to Melazarr. Melazarr looked up at her with confused, lion-like eyes.

"You stay here, you'll be safe. I'll be back for you. Don't move."

Melazarr stood, teetering a little.

"Don't move." Stenibelle hugged her and departed, crawling back into the vent.

Faded, Stenibelle headed for the rear hold. Just hours before she reasoned she couldn't stand over the bulk of the crew, but now she would have to. She was determined to protect the crew from Deckard, to delay her, to interdict her. Right now, Duval was busy re-writing the ship logs, making himself appear to be the wounded party. The crew was the proof of Duval's misconduct, they had to be protected.

All around, the ship throbbed and hummed with activity. Weapons discharged and reloaded. Incoming hits were taken. The ship banked hard. Groups of K-Listers moved about, getting into position. She watched them stow weapons into hidden drawers.

There was a massive crash and Stenibelle was nearly taken off her feet.

"Boarded!" The K-Listers mumbled amongst themselves. "Creation, we're boarded!" Others listened to portable Coms.

"We should we do?"

"The Marines have breached forward Deck 4! Captain says no hostile action. Surrender to them!"

"Why? So he can argue himself out of a jam before his own in the Admiralty and leave us to twist in the wind. Fuck that!" another said. "What about us? They'll have us sent to stockade on Olgolvy regardless. I say we fight and take a ripcar off the ship. We'll have the drop on them."

Stenibelle crawled out into the corridor. She heard the sounds of shouting and boots clomping about on the decks above. Soon a company of armed Marines appeared resplendent in their red uniforms.

"We give up!" the K-Listers said. They raised their hands in apparent surrender, while others in the back rows reached for their hidden weapons.

Faded, Stenibelle took great pleasure in ratting them out. "Marines, Marines, they are armed!!" she cried.

The K-Listers whirled about in a panic, looking for who spoke. They dove into any bit of cover they could find. Weapons came out. The Marines did likewise and a full-fledged gun battle took place, the two sides exchanging noisy SK and mixed caliber fire flecked with the distressed calls of people in pain, people crying for backup, people shouting oaths and other curses. Stenibelle dove out of the corridor. She heard pockets of gunfire erupt all over the ship. The *George Parr* had devolved into a desperate battleground. She felt confident the Marines, precision-trained and well-armed, would triumph in short order and locate Melazarr, taking her safely into custody. That was the best-case scenario for her. She was also confident that Captain Duval and Rodrigo of Burgon would soon be in Marine custody, she only wished she could be there to see it happen and laugh at them.

Now, time to preserve the evidence of his atrocities so that there would be little chance he could somehow talk his way out of this.

Time to save the crew.

13—REMM DECKARD

Stenibelle moved alone through the ship hearing the distant report of weapons firing. The lighting flickered and then went out all together. She shook up a yellow Holystone and continued through the dark.

A crack Marine squadron was now laying waste to Burgon and Duval's dreams. How lovely. They wanted the end of the universe, well here it is for them.

Ahead was the hold where she had rescued Lady Lessa. It flickered with emergency lighting. She heard the hydraulic drone of the loader in use peppered with the occasional thumps of containers being brought down to the floor. She tossed her Holystone aside.

She entered the hold. She saw the containers neatly stacked in tall columns in the center, each concealing a Shadow tech-poisoned female crewman. At the control desk was Remm Deckard, manipulating the loader, stacking the containers in the center. The ghoulish man Stenibelle had incapacitated and containered stood next to her, slightly wobbly from the lingering effects of the Pinkie. A slight orange glow from the screens at the desk danced about her face.

A warbling sound gave Stenibelle's presence away. All about the floor were a number of round glass nodules. The ones near her were flashing and making noise. Though invisible, her position was given up.

Deckard looked up from her work. She smiled. "Esther woman," she said. "Is that you? It must be."

"It's a demon," the man said wearily.

"Do shut up, will you?" Deckard replied.

She stepped out toward the containers and drew her knife from her Fleet coat. "I'm here to kill these people, Esther woman," she said. "I'm going to burn them up into nothing, and, I'm going to kill you too. Captain said to capture you, bring you back so they can brand you and make you their little slave. Funny thing, I don't see the Captain anywhere around, or the Xaphan. Captain's up there on Deck 2, surrendering to the Marines, talking his way out of trouble. So, I'm here to get rid of the evidence, and that includes you."

Stenibelle tried to move into a better position, the warblers on the floor gave her presence away again.

Deckard followed her movements with her eyes. "I know you're here. I still haven't figured out your stake in all of this? Will my killing these crew break your knee? Will it pick your pocket? What do you care? In another reality, Burgon said you're a man, here though, you're a sniveling little bitch wringing your hands and just waiting your turn to die. Why wait? Show yourself. Show yourself, or I'll burn everyone of them right now through their containers. Think I can't?"

Stenibelle didn't know what to do. If she had her gun, she'd just shoot her and be done with it. She decided to stall for time, for certainly the Marines would arrive soon and capture Deckard.

Stenibelle emerged from the shadows and they faced each other

Deckard smirked. "Well, well, you had the balls to show." She raised her knife.

Stenibelle flicked her wrists and had six MARZABLE daggers between her fingers. "I'll not let you hurt these people any further. I am here to protect them."

The man raised a heat gun. "I'll kill ya' for putting me up in that box!" Stenibelle let fly with three of her daggers, getting the man in the arm and chest. He fell with a cry and backed away.

"That man needs Hospitaler attention," she said.

"Does he?" Deckard turned to the man and slit his throat without hesitation.

Remm Deckard reared back and laughed. "That's how you get things done! You might be some Extra-Planar creature, whatever that is, but I am Famora from Moedron, and if you want to live you fight for it. Go ahead, take a shot, I give you a free opportunity to kill me. You'll not have another."

Stenibelle didn't hesitate, she let fly with her MARZABLE, throwing three of them as hard as she could. They found their mark, two in the chest and one right between the eyes.

All three bounced off with a distinct metallic CLUNK! CLUNK! CLUNK!

Deckard didn't flinch. "Ha! Do you see now what Moedron did to us? We are Famora and we are Once-Human. Let me show you!"

Before Stenibelle's eyes came a white-hot flash and a blast of terrible heat. Deckard had transformed into an effigy of fire, her clothes vaporizing and her knife turning to white hot in her hand. The dead man nearby caught fire. The temperature sensors squealed.

Deckard laughed, her voice a high-pitched sizzle. "You see, we are Famora, People of the Fire. The crew are being incinerated alive right through their containers right now. There won't even be ash when I'm done, just vapor. When the Marines get here they will find nothing. They will carry the day on the ship, but the captain will win the war. He'll be dragged off to the Fleet, and the admirals will dangle him before the gallows. He'll say pretty things. He'll blame the Marines and the scouting ship out there for the loss of life, all the missing crew. And he'll talk his way back onto the ship, and then he can do what he wants with the universe. I'll be there at his side. I'll remake Moedron into a paradise, into the best of places. In any universe, I am Famora."

The heat Deckard created was fierce, and Stenibelle could barely look at her without squinting—her eyeballs felt like they were melting. From what she could see, Deckard looked like a flaming iron billet on an anvil, splotchy oranges mixed with angry reds and fiery yellows dappled with bluish streaks of carbon imperfections and sparks of slag. Her eyes and her teeth were dark hammered splotches on her face and her hair was a veil of fire. Super-heated breath snorted from her furnace-like mouth.

There was a great shock that rumbled through the ship, knocking them both off their feet. The second Marine ship had breached the ship.

Deckard recovered and came at Stenibelle, darting with her ugly knife. Stenibelle shrunk from the heat. She couldn't cope with it. What was she to do? She flashed her daggers and instinctively met Deckard's knife, trying to protect herself. Deckard fought with glee, she seemed to want to torture Stenibelle, to make her suffer before finally killing her. She pushed her daggers aside and attacked with a terrible bear hug, wrapping her flaming arms around her, hoping to roast her alive.

Stenibelle withered in the heat, trying to cry out but unable to make a sound. Deckard laughed and squeezed tighter. Stenibelle jammed her daggers into her gut. It was like trying to stab an iron statue.

"Die . . . just die, like you were never even here. . ." Deckard hissed with glee.

Stenibelle thought to give in, to die here on the *George Parr*, to never see her family again, her father, her sisters, never see A-Ram and Alesta again.

To die along with the rest of the crew and never see Gwen again.

I have many questions.

I see you . . .

Gwen . . .

She played one last card.

BONG!!

The VUNKULA dashed out of her HRN and tagged Deckard hard on the chin. She recoiled and fell to one knee, stunned.

Free, Stenibelle backed up a step or two. She looked herself over, expecting to behold the charred ruins of her body. Instead, she saw nothing, no singeing, no blackened flesh or burnt hair. Her HRN wasn't even dirtied.

Her HRN??

Her HRN, infused with power from the Sisters, so she'd been told, seemed to have protected her from Deckard's furnace-like heat. While she didn't like the heat much, it wasn't hurting her.

Back in our Universe, the Sisters did something to the HRN, A-Ram had said.

Deckard stood and Stenibelle balled the Hoban Warclub on the end of her VUNKULA into a fist. The two squared off.

Deckard flashed her knife, Stenibelle turned it. She tried to bear hug Stenibelle again. She pushed Deckard away with two MARZABLE, and then, Stenibelle attacked.

BONG!!

Out came the VUNKULA with a terrible shot to Deckard's chest, creating a flurry of embers and shed bits of carbon. Deckard seemed puzzled, possibly stunned a second time. She came again.

BONG!! Another hammering blow from the VUNKULA.

BONG!! Another.

BONG!! And another. The VUNKULA moved like a wrecking ball, hitting Deckard one way, and then coming back the next. Left, right, the pounding took its toll. Deckard was losing confidence, her fire going out, no longer looking to attack, now she pulled back, trying to defend herself from the onslaught, looking for a route to flee. Stenibelle gave her no pause, landing hammer shot and hammer shot. Her flame darkened, her body turning black. Deckard dropped her knife, it hissed on the floor.

Stenibelle wasted no time gloating. She remained silent, and took Deckard apart one blow at a time, pounding her like a blacksmith working a billet of iron.

Deckard turned to run. Stenibelle hit her again, knocking her jaw off. She fell and her flame went out. Her steaming body lay there twisted up on the floor, like an iron statue forged all wrong, pounded into tormented deformity.

Several minutes later the first wave of Marines arrived. Hands up, Stenibelle greeted them. "I give up!" she cried. "And I would like to see Captain Gwendolyn right away."

swish, Knock, knock . . .

The battle aboard the *George Parr* was over. The Marines had carried the day.

Stenibelle stood in the hold where she had battled Remm Deckard. The Marines were in the process of transferring the crew from their cargo containers to proper medical capsules. They were then to be off-loaded to the Marine ships and taken to Bazz for immediate Hospitaler treatment. She watched the process. She had stood over them, and now she would see them off. As each capsule passed by, she gave them her Tyrol Wishluck gesture: a flourish with her fingers followed by two knocks.

"What are you doing?"

Lt. Gwendolyn stood next to her watching her swish and knock on each capsule.

"It's something we do in Tyrol, just wishing them luck and safe journey."

She felt Gwendolyn knock on her shoulder lightly and sweep with her fingers. Stenibelle smiled. "What was that for?"

"As you said, for luck."

"You did it backwards, but thank you."

"I spoke with Lady Lessa, Bel," Lt. Gwendolyn said. "The things she told me were quite unbelievable. She was quite hysterical and difficult to understand, truth be told, but, she verified what you had told me. So I set out right away and picked up two cutter ships loaned out from the 13th Marines. It was fortunate that the *George Parr* was sailing in the direction it was, otherwise, we'd not intercepted as quickly."

"Has Lady Lessa sought medical attention?"

"She has. She is under Hospitaler care on Planet Fall."

"How many are being taken out?" Stenibelle asked.

"Thirty-six. All safe, thanks to you. How are you, Bel? Are you all right?"

"I'm fine, Gwen, I . . ." Stenibelle saw the concern on Gwen's face. "I'm fine. I'm rather tired."

"Then you must go to my ship where you can rest. I've set aside quarters for you."

"What about Hold 4. What was found there?"

"Nothing. The Marines performed a complete inspection. They found nothing but a bit of earth and a few piles of cinders. They did detect Shadow tech in the hold, but could find no source."

"The Punts there must have fled the ship somehow, and they took the statue with them. No matter, they are gone. I would like to see Melazarr, where is she?"

"The Caroline woman? The giant?"

"The very one. She is rather tall, isn't she?"

"She's down this way, I think," Gwen said pointing. "It's not good news."

They exited the hold and went down the corridor, passing groups of Marines and dispirited pockets of captured K-Listers who had happened to survive the battle. Around the bend was a makeshift and somewhat grisly morgue. Bodies of fallen K-Listers were piled up, being identified. Some were being put into bags. A few Marines were wounded and receiving field treatment.

Down the way Stenibelle saw a slender pair of feet and long legs supine, mixed in with the dead K-Listers.

Stenibelle winced. She walked up and looked down at Melazarr's still body among the dead. "Get up, please," she said. "This is no place for you."

Melazarr opened her yellow eyes and sat up. She held her arms out and Stenibelle helped her up, Gods but was she heavy. She was wearing a donated Marine coat over her tiny robe and a hat, though her legs and feet were still bare. She seemed to have recovered a spark of her wits from Burgon's drugs, and bits of her personality were showing through. She appeared to be a winsome, adventurous person, full of life and curiosity. Stenibelle was looking forward to getting to know her, to hearing her speak and the stories she had to tell.

Certainly a Xaphan Tropist would have a host of lurid tales to regale her with.

"She really shouldn't be wandering off and laying down with the dead," Gwendolyn said. "There could be K-Listers lurking about unaccounted for. We should get her aboard my ship immediately. She needs to be properly dressed and shoed. By Creation, she's half naked."

"Burgon liked her that way. The drugs he plied her with seem to be wearing off."

"We'll have a Hospitaler look her over and give a proper diagnosis. Xaphan potions can be long-lasting with significant side-effects. We need to make certain she's healthy."

"Has she been checked for any Xaphan assassination devices or poisons? I don't trust Burgon."

"The Marines performed a field check on her. She had a Midas Chastity Key brand which was removed. They didn't find anything else."

"He tried to brand me with one of those and I wasn't having it. Gwen, may I see Captain Duval? I need something he took."

"What did he take?"

"A chart. Just a memento, but it's important to me and I must have it."

"He's in his quarters under guard. So is the Xaphan. As soon as my orders come down from Fleet, we'll be moving him to the brig aboard my ship. We have to be careful in these matters and follow correct procedure. Taking a captain off his flagged vessel is a complicated process. We don't wish him having anything on which to build a case for defense. We have him dead to rights on a staggering number of violations and I'd hate to see him slither out of it on a minor technicality. Such things have happened before."

"Then I must see him, now please."

Gwendolyn nodded. "If you must." They walked down the corridor and headed into the lift. Melazarr tried to pad behind them and follow but Stenibelle asked her to stay with the Marines where she would be safe.

The lift door closed and they went up. "We just completed purging the deck of V-Trax gas," Gwendolyn said. "There might be some lingering pockets. You must tell me if you feel ill."

"Will you feel its effects?"

"I'm immune to it. I've been inoculated."

Stenibelle looked up at her face. "I'm eager to discuss certain matters with you later, the picture and so on, if that still interests you."

Gwen blushed a little and said nothing. Stenibelle barely knew Gwendolyn, yet she felt perfectly at ease, as if she'd known her for years, and Gwendolyn herself seemed more engaged, less submerged in her loneliness.

"I could see you hiding in the tailoring office," Gwendolyn said. "I was relieved that you were unharmed."

Stenibelle felt invigorated by her presence. A-Ram and Alesta had said Gwen as a *Merthig* gave her power, and she certainly felt it. She longed to kiss Gwendolyn, as she had on Planet Fall, but this time not in anger. But she hid the thought. It certainly wasn't proper.

"How's your watch," Stenibelle asked.

"It's still working."

The doors opened. The finery of Deck 2 was in shambles. Bullet and energy blasts riddled the walls, bloodstains marred the floor. She smelled the sweet notes of V-Trax floating around. A company of Marines stood guard. Gwendolyn led her down the deck and into Duval's quarters. Inside, Duval and Burgon sat on a couch flanked by Marine guards. Duval saw Stenibelle and smiled.

"Ah, Lady Stenibelle. No worse for your adventures, I see. I was concerned for your safety."

"Were you? I saw Remm Deckard in the hold. I don't know if she is alive or dead."

"So, I take it you assaulted my First Officer, who was in the process of establishing parlay with the Marines to ensure no lives were lost. No doubt your actions caused the tragic and unnecessary misunderstanding here that cost many lives. Good to know, and I thank you for that talking point."

"She was attempting to murder the crew, under your orders."

Duval shrugged. "I issued no such orders. Very bad business about the crew. Fell victim to this Xaphan's plot. I wish I'd uncovered it sooner."

Duval was a slick character, even now he was working on his defense, turning on Burgon. Burgon himself sat there and seemed a dejected and beaten man.

"I want the chart Melazarr drew, Duval. Give it to me," Stenibelle said.

Hearing her name, Burgon shuffled in his seat. "Melazarr? Where is she?"

Duval spoke over him. "That chart is my personal property, Lady Stenibelle. Are you hoping to steal it from me, in front of all these witnesses? If you must know, it is in my right breast pocket and that is where it will stay."

Stenibelle approached.

"Of course, you realize you cannot touch me, or steal my things. Such matter could assist in my defense, as I truthfully build the case that I am an innocent pawn, my ship hijacked, my goods stolen, my person assaulted. It's a wonder I survived to be rescued by the Marines at all."

"Well then, it's a good thing the chart doesn't belong to you, does it? It belongs to Melazarr of Caroline, written by her hand on vellum belonging to Rodrigo of Burgon, signed with her name. It's a good thing Burgon here corroborates my story. It's a good thing he is thinking of his defense as well."

She turned to him. "Right, Burgon?"

Burgon made no reply.

The VUNKULA emerged from Stenibelle's coat and gingerly dipped into Duval's. Before he could react, she had the chart. The VUNKULA slid back into the depths of her HRN. "I'll just take that back and return it to her. There, it's also a good thing I didn't touch you in the matter of returning Melazarr her things."

Burgon quietly spoke. "May I see Melazarr?"

"No."

"May I please see Melazarr?"

"No. You will not see her again."

He looked defeated and genuinely heartbroken. "I would have built her a whole world, filled with all the things she loves."

"Listen to this lunatic," Duval said. "Clearly deranged and quite Xaphan in his madness. How fortunate for us all the Marines put a stop to your plans."

Burgon wept, showing his teeth. "Have they?" he asked. He lifted his hand and gripped his right pinky with his left thumb and forefinger.

"Have they, Duval?" he repeated.

"What are you doing?" Duval asked, a slight note of alarm in his voice.

Burgon said a brief prayer to some pagan god.

"Marines! Marines! Shoot this man, he's—"

Burgon snapped his pinky, moving it into a grotesque position.

Instantly, his head exploded in a spray. Duval had a moment to suck in his breath, then his head exploded too, the two dead men knocking together headless on the couch. The Marines called out in shock. Gwendolyn came rushing into the room.

"Good Creation. Burgon must have infused the Captain with a Shadow tech Nyke poison! All he had to do is slip it into the Captain's coffee or tea. Very difficult to spot, and very effective!" Gwen said.

Stenibelle stared in horror at the two dead men on the couch, their dreams dashed aside in a spray of gore.

She had a terrible thought. If Burgon could have done that to the Captain, then certainly he could have done the same to Melazarr. She exited the room.

She had to be all right. She just had to. She went down the lift, looking for Melazarr.

There was a commotion in the corridor ahead. She grit her teeth and feared the worst, that perhaps Burgon had tainted Melazarr with the same Nyke poison, taking her with him in death.

There she was just ahead, standing tall in her borrowed red coat, dancing with a Marine.

She breathed a heavy sigh of relief. "Melazarr, thank Creation. I was worried."

The Marines turned to Stenibelle. Blood coated their faces. Melazarr had no head. Several of the Marines were covered in her blood. One of them, in shock, was holding her up.

Burgon had killed her too. What had A-Ram and Alesta said: the *Merten* was difficult to keep alive. Try as one might, the Universe would see them dead.

They were correct.

14—Prentiss

The carriage stopped near the main entrance of the country manor. Stenibelle hopped out and allowed her HRN to furl around her. She picked up the small package and held in it in both hands. Inside, resting in a cushioned box, was a fine crystal for a ladies watch; rare and expensive.

She crunched across the gravel toward the door to Prentiss Manor holding the box. Stenibelle smiled, bursting with joy as the door neared.

Much had happened to bring her to this place. Much had happened since the battle on the *George Parr*.

Stenibelle gave the chart Melazarr had made to Hannah-Ben Shurlamp, and she confirmed the data were good. Great acclaim came to her. Cammara rediscovered! Talks of assembling an armada to go there were already under way. A *Ritchie*-class scout ship was christened in her honor, ready to go to Cammara that she had rediscovered. Hannah-Ben Shurlamp broke open the bottle on the ship's nose, a slight smile on her face.

Professor Shurlamp had promised her riches, and she came through. The heir she promised surfaced, and the man was married to Stenibelle's sister, Ione. The House of Belmont-South Tyrol was saved, and mysterious money flowed into its coffers. The House thrived once again.

Stenibelle returned Melazarr's body to her ancestral grounds in Hala by the sea and buried her there in a sun-washed grave deep in the green. She often felt the need to go out there and sit with her, to keep her company. She wished she hadn't died, she cursed the Universe for that.

Of A-Ram and Alesta, she saw them one more time. She showed them the chart, and they scanned an image of it and said her mission was done, the rest of it was for others to perform. Weeping, they embraced her and she never saw them again—at least those versions of A-Ram and Alesta. She tracked down A-Ram in the Fleet HQ, but he was a different A-Ram, not the same one who she had come to cherish as a friend. They apparently, belonged to another Universe. She supposed other aspects of herself out there somewhere were, even now, hard at it and under their guidance. She found herself envying them a little—what adventures they must be experiencing.

And she missed the A-Ram and Alesta she had come to know. This version of A-Ram lacked something the other had—verve, life and a wonderful woman at his side. He was so shy and blinking behind his thick lenses. She knew what was ailing him—he was missing Alesta. She had loved seeing them together, their love was infectious and inclusive, had the warm feel of family. This A-Ram, the A-Ram of her universe, seemed incomplete, rather like Gwendolyn had seemed incomplete. Still, she managed through persistence to cultivate a sedate but growing friendship with him. Slowly, he opened up to her, revealing small glimpses of the A-Ram she knew. Her goal was to locate Lady Alesta out there somewhere in the vastness of the League and introduce them, bring them together—it was a gift she wanted to give to them. They loved each other in another universe, and they could do so here as well. She longed for the moment where she could witness them together for the first time, watching the opening flicker of their love form before her eyes. They seemed meant for each other, and they had helped make her into a new woman. She would search for Lady Alesta even if it took years.

She kept tabs on Lady Lessa of Walpole to see how she was doing. She recovered from her ordeal aboard the *George Parr* and conscripted about another ship, the *Master Fax*. After a period of mourning, she became engaged to another man. Stenibelle wished her well.

As for Julia of Fountain-Lock, Stenibelle wondered and wondered what had become of her, running around naked with her pink hair on Planet Fall. She bought wall space on several Public Panels on Hoffman Plate and placed an ad with the title JULIA LOVES ????, entreating Julia of Fountain-Locke to get in touch with her. She didn't have to wait long. A few weeks after the *George Parr*, Stenibelle received a payment-due message from Hoffman Plate, Planet Fall. It was Julia, living virtually naked on the streets. Starving and desperate, she asked Stenibelle for some money to buy food, some clothes and a freightliner ticket to return home to Tubruk. She said she didn't have anyone else to ask.

Checking up on her, Stenibelle found that Julia indeed appeared to be all alone. Her family on Tubruk had all but disavowed her as a wayward, disaffected daughter. She had no friends that Stenibelle could find, she was the reject of several convents on Tubruk, and she was indelibly etched into the K-List of the Fleet.

She was truly a person with no place to go.

Instead, Stenibelle sent for her and gave her a room at Belmont Manor. Stenibelle was strict with her: no piercings, no pink hair, and no drugs or alcohol. She also made her get rid of the 4D tattoo pointing at her crotch. Julia was moody and rebellious and was like a petulant child given to fits of temper and vandalism. She spray painted her room and shredded the clothes Stenibelle had bought for her. Stenibelle was not going to give up on her. She dragged her down to the sand pit for a few sessions, she made her re-paint her room and also made her work in the kitchens everyday for several months. Her goal was to clean Julia up, screw her head on straight and transform her into a proper young lady. As the pink came out replaced with tawny brown, she did respond She no longer vandalized her room, she did her chores in the kitchens without complaint, and, even though she was only a few years younger than Stenibelle, she called her "Mom". She planned to send her off to school to Traveler or the University of Dee so that she could learn a skill, make something of herself and go off and start a family of her own.

The life she saved would not be wasted. Gods, Stenibelle thought, *I sound like my mother . . .*

Epilogue

Here I am at last, come to the place where I have always meant to be. I have come to know that I exist in many places, mostly as a man, a rogue, an eccentric, a man of the Sisters bearing their power.

In many places I am a great man.

And, I have also come to know that in this particular place, I am a great woman, no less of stature than anywhere else. At last, I am at peace with my brothers from afar, and with myself. I contribute my strength to theirs.

I have learned much.

I am a woman who has learned to value and cherish my friends, I have learned to rely upon myself and value the skills that I have and take confidence that I am great.

And, most of all, I am a woman who has learned to follow her heart, wherever it may lead.

Here it has led me.

I told you once, Gwen, that I am not the man who loved you in a different place. Your heart broke, I felt it break and mine broke with you. But, look at me, I am the same person as those other men with the same soul finally allowed to shine, and the love I feel and have come to accept is no different than theirs.

Here I am, Gwen, gone for too long, but not forgotten. Not quite the person you were expecting, but full of love just the same. My heart has led me here, and we needn't be alone ever again.

Here, as elsewhere, we belong to each other.

AUTHOR INFORMATION

Ren Garcia is a Science Fiction/Fantasy author and Texas native who grew up in western Ohio. He has been writing since before he could write, often scribbling alien lingo on any available wall or floor with assorted crayons. He attended The Ohio State University and majored in English Literature. Ren has been an avid lover of anything surreal since childhood. He also has a passion for caving, urban archaeology and architecture. He currently lives in Columbus, Ohio with his wife, and their four dogs.